I0763989

MANGLER BOOK 5: THE SEWER DISTRICT

STEVEN GALE

DEDICATION

To Hannah, Aaron, and my wife Sally.
To our five grandkids:
DREAM BIG AND DARE TO FAIL.

First paperback edition May 2026
First ebook edition May 2026
Print ISBN: 979-8-9941452-2-7
Ebook ISBN: 979-8-9941452-3-4

Book cover and interior design by JohnEdgar.Design
Published by Agragape Publications

MISS CANDY
BURLES
REVUE

STEVEN GALE

STORYTELLER & AUTHOR

As a child, Steven would hide behind his dad's chair while watching the TV show 'The Night Stalker.' Growing up during what many consider the best era in film history, he believes this experience helped shape his imagination and storytelling abilities. He feels that today's special effects have deprived people of the opportunity to develop their own creative imaginations.

Steven is the father of two veterans and the husband of a wonderful wife. He is an avid golfer and enjoys hiking in the mountains.

MANGLER BOOK 5: THE SEWER DISTRICT

STEVEN GALE

CONTENTS

PROLOGUE

The Sewer District is the largest prison system in both known and unknown worlds. It functions as an underground city, beneath Atlantis, divided into five zones, each separated by a river. Access to The Sewer District is through two sets of elevators located in an ancient church, whose age and history hint at secrets and stories waiting to be uncovered. One elevator is designated for visitors, while the larger one is used to transport prisoners. The church leads into Zone One, known as the Lower Zone, which then connects to Zone Two, called the Capital Zone. From there, it continues to Zone Three, referred to as the Prison Zone. Next is Zone Four, called the Utility Zone, and finally, Zone Five, known as the Upper Zone. In this underground prison, water from Atlantis above constantly falls from the ceiling like rain.

Hybrids are said to be descended from fallen angels, as described in the Bible. These beings are the offspring of fallen angels and human women. They possess a striking blend of divine and human traits, making them stand out as giants or formidable warriors.

MANGLER
BOOK 5

THE SEWER DISTRICT

Don't be afraid to get lost, because that's where the adventures begin.

Unknown

CHAPTER ONE

THE BATTLE CHESS GAME

1725 HOURS
PRESENT-DAY
SPORTS DISTRICT, ATLANTIS

The afternoon is buzzing with anticipation as the Battle Chess championship draws to a thrilling climax tonight. Doyle and his father, Barry, are deeply immersed in the contest from their luxurious skybox, perched high above the intricately designed chessboard below. Doyle, still recovering from a recent mission that left him with a knee injury, sports a sturdy knee brace, but that doesn't dampen his excitement. He takes a refreshing sip of his cool drink, leaning eagerly over the polished handrail, his head half-extending out of the skybox to catch every detail of the unfolding drama.

Below, the atmosphere is charged as a group of AI medics rushes to assist a chess bishop who the opposing team's fierce queen has just defeated. The bishop, a strong knight in his own right, clutches a towel to his forehead in a futile attempt to stem the flow of blood, making his way off the board with a mix of pride and weariness etched into his chiseled features.

Barry glances at Doyle, a look of exhilaration on his face. "That was an incredible fight! These Battle Chess matches can match the excitement of octagon fights back in America," he exclaims, his voice filled with enthusiasm for the spectacle they are witnessing.

Doyle smiles and says, "It's really impressive! I can't believe how strong the queens are. Those women are just as powerful as the men, even though they're smaller and, might I add, beautiful women."

"Totally! The Battle Chess League has some interesting rules, though. They don't allow hybrids; players need to be at least eighty percent human," Barry explains.

"I'd say the queens are pretty much right at that limit, maybe even exactly eighty percent!" Doyle adds, looking intrigued.

"Gentlemen!" Jonah exclaimed, his voice echoing with excitement as he stepped into the luxurious skybox. The atmosphere inside was vibrant, charged with the thrill of the tournament. "What a magnificent tournament this has been! I understand you two have been here the entire weekend."

"Afternoon, Jonah," Doyle replied with a casual nod, a hint of camaraderie in his tone.

Barry, his expression a mix of surprise and warmth, waved at Jonah. "What brings you up here, my friend?"

Jonah reached for a frosty drink from the attentive skybox waitress, the coolness refreshing his senses. "I need to have a word with Doyle about his next mission," he said, his tone shifting to one of seriousness.

"That's what I figured as soon as I saw you enter," Doyle said, sliding his chair across the polished floor to make space for Jonah, who then settled into a chair, his expression focused.

"Thank you," Jonah said, taking his seat and opening up a sleek digital notebook. "We need to discuss the details of this mission."

Doyle leaned in, a knowing smile on his face. "Go ahead; I'm all ears."

Just then, the crowd erupted in cheers and gasps. Barry stood up, captivated by a fierce clash unfolding on the chessboard. A pawn and a knight were locked in a stunning duel, each piece embodying strategy and fierce determination. With a decisive move, the knight struck, sending the pawn tumbling to the ground as it tapped out, eliciting a deafening roar from the audience.

"That was quite the fight," Jonah remarked, momentarily distracted by the excitement. He turned his attention back to Doyle, his expression serious. "We've received troubling reports of a flying disk that has crashed on an uninhabited island west of Atlantis."

"What could have caused it to crash? I thought that was impossible," Doyle questioned, furrowing his brow in concern.

Jonah locked eyes with Doyle, urgency radiating from his expression. "I wish it were impossible, but unfortunately, it's not. The disk was flying at low altitude when it either experienced a critical malfunction or was potentially shot down. The precise circumstances surrounding the incident remain ambiguous, and we won't have clear answers until we can deploy a team to the crash site. Regrettably, we've been unable to establish any form of contact with the pilots or the officers aboard the disk."

"What type of mission were they undertaking?" Doyle pressed, his brow furrowing with concern.

Jonah glanced down at his detailed notes before responding, "They were on a diplomatic mission to an island located just north of their current position. The crash site is shrouded in dense jungle, characterized by towering trees and thick underbrush, and it is known to be home to a variety of large and aggressive wildlife."

"Do you think they survived the crash?" Doyle inquired, concern evident in his tone.

"Yes, we have strong reasons to believe they did. However, this island is well known for its strong magnetic field, which disrupts most electronic devices, rendering communication devices ineffective. Consequently, they currently lack a means to reach out for assistance," Jonah articulated thoughtfully.

"That certainly complicates matters without communication," Doyle acknowledged.

"It does. However, that's why we have you on our team, an expert in search and rescue. I am confident, based on your extensive background, that you've successfully navigated many missions without communication, and I believe you will excel in this situation as well," Jonah stated.

Doyle nodded in agreement. "I have indeed, on more occasions than I can count."

At that moment, a group of individuals entered the skybox, accompanied by a tall, four-armed hybrid wearing green-tinted glasses. The hybrid turned to Jonah and extended a hand in greeting. "Mr. Jonah, it's a pleasure to see you. How have you been?"

"I'm doing well, thank you, Counselor Folly," Jonah responded as he rose to acknowledge him.

"Excellent to hear. I came to meet the remarkable super soldier you've enlisted. His name, if I'm not mistaken, is Anderson," Folly remarked.

"I'm Doyle. Doyle Anderson," Doyle introduced himself as he approached Folly with a welcoming demeanor.

"Good to meet you, Doyle," Folly said warmly, offering a firm handshake that conveyed confidence and assurance.

"Same here," Doyle replied, a hint of curiosity in his voice as he took in the unfamiliar figure.

Folly then turned his attention to Jonah, his expression serious. "I gathered from our morning assembly that a flying disk encountered some trouble and went down. I want you to know that I'm here to help in any way you might need."

"Thank you, Counselor," Jonah acknowledged, appreciating the offer in light of recent events.

The glimmer of challenge in the Counselor's eyes was unmistakable as he turned to Doyle, his voice rich with the weight of shared history. "I understand that Deborah deliberately chose to accompany you on your perilous mission to dismantle the treacherous tunnel that leads to the isolated fortress of Dr. Frucus's island. We shared countless hours of companionship and camaraderie before her life was shattered by the brutal injustice that saw her framed and confined within the grim walls of The Sewer District."

Jonah interrupted, his tone sharp as he coughed to clear his throat, determination etched on his face. "She was not framed. Her trial was a long and arduous ordeal, stretching over many months, and she was given the sentence that she thoroughly deserved."

With a mocking laugh that reverberated like thunder in the charged atmosphere, the Counselor sneered, "And who appointed you as the ultimate judge of morality? Who granted you the authority to pass judgment on the choices of others?" His voice dripped with condescension, slicing through the tension like a sharpened blade.

Jonah, unable to contain his exasperation any longer, retorted with increasing fervor, "This is neither the appropriate time nor the right place for this debate, Counselor!" His voice resonated off the sleek, glass walls of the skybox, emphasizing the urgency of the moment.

"Very good," Folly replied, a sardonic smile curling his lips as he nodded slightly. He turned on his heel and strode confidently out of the skybox, his demeanor radiating superiority. His small entourage followed closely, their footsteps a muted echo in the expansive, modern room, in contrast to the intensity of the prior exchange.

As the heavy door sealed shut behind them with a resounding click, Doyle leaned forward, curiosity illuminating his expression. "Who was that peculiar man?" he inquired, his eyebrows knitting together in confusion.

Jonah raised a hand, gesturing for everyone to settle back into their seats, the weight of his words palpable in the charged air. "He's a counselor from the affluent political district uptown," he began, his voice steady yet layered with caution. "He has well-documented ties to the infamous MIA gang operating in the labyrinthine underbelly of the Sewer District, although he's always quick to dispute any allegations of involvement. His reputation precedes him; he's infamous as one of the most corrupt attorneys in all of Atlantis, adept at wielding his considerable influence like a double-edged sword."

The crowd erupted into a symphony of cheers and applause as the black chess team masterfully executed a checkmate against their white opponents, the tension charged in the air. Jonah sprang to his feet, his eyes shining with excitement, clapping vigorously as his voice rose above the din. "I absolutely love this version of chess! The strategic battles unfold like a gripping drama. It adheres strictly to the original chess rules about checks and checkmates; once you're in check, there's no fighting your way out, you must move to block the check call."

Doyle, clearly caught up in the electric atmosphere, stood up beside him, his enthusiasm infectious. With a broad smile, he added, "It's undeniably addictive! The thrill of each move is far more captivating than American football!" His words resonated with the crowd, who were equally swept up in the game's energy.

After the crowd quieted, Jonah and Doyle settled back into their seats, the air thick with tension. "The Counselor has four sons, each intricately entwined in the shadowy empire he has meticulously crafted. They are notorious figures, cloaked in secrecy and whispers, if you're curious about the darker aspects of their nature. The eldest, Edward, is particularly unsettling. Rumors swirl that he cultivates a portion of his illicit drugs on the very island where our flying disk met its tragic fate. He was married to Deborah for many years, and together they welcomed a son into a world rife with danger and despair," Jonah revealed, his voice laden with the gravity of the information.

"A son, really? Where is he now?" Doyle inquired, a deep frown creasing his forehead as he struggled to process the weight of the situation.

Jonah shook his head slowly, a storm cloud of concern shadowing his features. "We have him in protective custody. Edward, driven to the brink by his violent tendencies, has vowed to kill him if he ever manages to track him down."

"That's absolutely insane," Doyle replied, disbelief tinging his voice.

Jonah nodded thoughtfully, his brow furrowed. "Indeed, he is a distraught soul, as I've stated before. Beneath his ruthless exterior lies a chilling, grotesque deformity: six elongated fingers on each hand, giving him an almost monstrous visage and an unsettling reminder of his erratic behavior. In stark contrast, the Counselor's youngest son, Augustine, has chosen a treacherous path of his own—he leads the infamous MIA gang, a shadowy organization operating in the murky depths of the Sewer District, where danger lurks in every shadow and alley. His deformity is equally bizarre, marked by three vivid, ever-watchful eyes that seem to perceive everything and nothing all at once, a haunting gaze that unsettles even the most hardened of souls."

Doyle shook his head in disbelief as the gravity of the situation sank in. "He really trained his sons to become criminals, huh? What about the other two boys?"

Jonah took a deep breath, his voice steady yet laced with concern. "They, too, have followed in their father's dubious footsteps and are entrenched in the drug trade. They operate from two smaller, remote islands nestled northwest of Atlantis, which are firmly under their control. However, these two brothers, August and Donor, prefer to maintain a lower profile; they are far more cautious and seem somewhat intimidated by their surroundings. Their reluctance to expose themselves ensures that you won't see much of them out in public."

They sat in contemplative silence, the rhythmic click of brooms echoing from below as the board was meticulously cleaned and arranged for the next match. Jonah leaned in closer to Doyle, the dim light casting shadows across his serious expression, and spoke in a hushed, urgent voice. "We need to go over some critical details about this mission—you can't underestimate its importance. You'll need to assemble a small but capable team, one that is resourceful and trustworthy, to help you track down the crashed flying disk and locate the officers who were aboard. Once you reach the crash site, your objective is unequivocal: plant explosives on that flying disk to obliterate it. We cannot afford to let that advanced technology fall into the wrong hands. Let's hope the officers are safe and somewhere in the vicinity, still able to assist you."

Doyle's brow furrowed deeply, concern etched into his features as he considered the implications. "But what if they're not in that area? What if they're lost or captured?"

Jonah nodded gravely, his eyes reflecting the seriousness of the situation. "In that case, you will have no choice but to find them. You must understand one crucial detail about this island: while it may seem like a barren, uninhabited landscape at first glance, it hides a wealth of secrets and dangers. The MIA gang has transformed this remote paradise into a concealed drug farm, shrouded in shadows and deceit. I can assure you, treacherous booby traps are likely to be lurking at every turn, ready to ensnare the unwary and complicate your already hazardous search."

As he concluded his remarks, the weight of their mission hung over the room, each carefully chosen word resonating with the stark reality of the dangers that lay ahead.

"Understood. Where do I begin assembling my team?" Doyle inquired, his voice steady yet tinged with an edge of apprehension.

"You can select the same individuals you rallied from the Sewer District," Jonah replied, a flicker of optimism brightening his expression. "I have no doubt Deborah will be eager to lend her support for this undertaking."

Doyle let out a light chuckle, shaking his head with a hint of resignation. "Let's face it, helping me definitely isn't her primary concern. However, I must admit, her expertise will be crucial for this particular mission."

Jonah nodded, a knowing smile illuminating his face. "She truly embodies an indomitable spirit. Beneath that strong-willed facade lies an extraordinary warrior, renowned for unmatched skill. Unfortunately, we can't seem to muster many more individuals like her on our side."

Doyle sat observing the expansive arena, his gaze drifting across the vibrant scene, when something caught his attention. Directly across from him in a lavish skybox was Counselor Folly, a striking figure whose intense stare was fixed on Doyle like a hawk focused on its prey. The Counselor's brow was deeply furrowed, indicating his concentration and perhaps a hint of anger.

In the skybox with him were two peculiar companions. One was a bizarre creature with a large, square head that seemed to rest directly on its broad shoulders, with no visible neck. Its dark red skin gleamed under the arena lights, giving it an otherworldly appearance. The second individual stood to the Counselor's left and was even more eccentric; his eyes humorously perched atop long, thin pipe cleaners that soared nearly a foot above his head, making him look as if he had just stepped out of a surreal painting.

Together, the three stared at Doyle with unsettling, expressionless faces, their silence amplifying the bizarre atmosphere around them.

The arena came alive with a dazzling display of flashing lights, illuminating the faces of eager spectators packed into every corner. A powerful voice resonated through the sound system, commanding attention: "Ladies and gentlemen, and hybrids from the farthest reaches of the lands unburdened by ice, I proudly present to you the climactic final match of the semi-finals! Join me in giving a thunderous welcome to our two exceptional teams! Representing the black team, we have the daring and strategic Team Gibbs, and taking the squares for the white team is the astute and agile Team Lux."

The crowd erupted into a cacophony of cheers and applause, their excitement reverberating throughout the arena as the two teams confidently strode onto the vast chessboard, meticulously marked with alternating black and white squares. Each player assumed their positions with an air of focus and intensity, ready to engage in the battle of wits and strength.

The king of Team White, adorned in a majestic crown glistening with jewels and a flowing robe that cascaded around him like a river of silk, captivated all present. His voice rose above the clamor of the crowd, resonating with authority as he proclaimed, "E-4!" In response, the pawn stationed directly before him surged forward with boldness, gliding two squares into the heart of the battlefield with purpose. This decisive move signaled the dawn of an enthralling contest, brimming with intricate strategies and fierce rivalries. The air crackled with excitement and anticipation, as spectators leaned forward, eager for the unfolding drama that promised a riveting clash of intellect and skill.

The king of Team Black, undeterred, mirrored this bold maneuver by playing E-4 as well, establishing a fierce parity. Team White then strategically repositioned its knight to F3, laying the early groundwork for its game plan.

"They're opting for the Italian Game strategy," Barry remarked to his son, his voice a mix of admiration and intrigue.

Doyle nodded thoughtfully, his eyes fixed on the board. "Looks that way, Dad." The tension in the arena was palpable as each player engaged in a cerebral battle destined to captivate all who watched.

Jonah smiled warmly as he watched the two men reveling in the electrifying atmosphere of the match, a moment of joy that both of them desperately needed. With a friendly pat on Doyle's back, he stated, "You guys have a great time, but I have to head out now. Tomorrow at 0900, I'll meet you at the elevator for the Sewer District on your apartment floor. Does that work for you?"

Doyle stood up, a hint of excitement in his eyes, and took Jonah's hand in a firm shake. "See you then," he replied, just as the crowd erupted in cheers, their voices a tidal wave of energy as the first fight of the new match kicked off.

"Hit him!" Barry shouted, springing to his feet, his face lit with enthusiasm as the action unfolded in the ring.

Jonah stepped out of the sleek, modern skybox, the glass walls offering a breathtaking panoramic view of the vibrant arena below. The bustling crowd buzzed with energy, a stark contrast to the skybox's calm. He spotted Mike leaning against the polished black railing, his relaxed posture belying an alertness as he surveyed the distant horizon where the sky met the earth.

"Mike, we need to contact Deborah and inform her that Doyle will be stopping by in the morning," Jonah said, his voice steady but laced with urgency, the weight of the moment hanging in the air.

“I'll handle it right away,” Mike replied, a deep furrow creasing his forehead. His sharp eyes darted to the entrance. “By the way, did I just see Counselor Folly slip out of the skybox a moment ago?”

Jonah's expression darkened, the flicker of anger igniting in his gaze. “Yes. That man never misses an opportunity to harass me. I have a strong suspicion he's somehow involved in the disk crash we just experienced. He never drops by unannounced, yet here he was, appearing on the very day we face a significant failure. We need to brief the team; the pilots and officers might be held hostage by his son, Edward, on that island.”

“I completely agree. I'll ensure Doyle is armed with the necessary weapons to tackle any threats he might encounter out there,” Mike responded, his voice resolute, determination etched across his features.

As they walked towards the sleek elevator that would transport them to the rooftop, where their high-tech flying car awaited against the backdrop of the sprawling city, Jonah paused, a contemplative expression shadowing his face. “Oh, and don't forget to instruct the shipmen to prepare the ship, the replica of the Queen Anne's Revenge pirate ship, for the voyage. We will need its capabilities in the shallow waters for this mission against the Krakens,” he added, a glint of concern shining brightly in his eyes as his mind raced with the daunting challenges that lay ahead.

As they stepped into the sleek, illuminated elevator, the soft whir of mechanisms surrounded them like a gentle embrace. Mike turned to Jonah, a grin lighting up his face. “Have you had the chance to tell Doyle about the Kraken yet?”

Jonah shifted his gaze to the back glass panel, where the breathtaking skyline of Atlantis unfolded before him. Majestic spires of shimmering glass and polished metal reached toward the heavens, reflecting vibrant hues of purple and blue from the twilight sky. Ahead, the skies were alive with a flurry of flying cars, their bright headlights slicing through the air, zipping past like colorful shooting stars.

"No," Jonah replied, a playful tone creeping into his voice. "I think I'll leave the job of breaking that news to Deborah. She has a talent for storytelling and knows how to make a grand entrance. I'm sure she'll capture his attention in a way that I couldn't."

"Yeah, she has a way with words," Mike replied as he and Jonah walked out of the elevator and climbed into their flying car.

The advanced AI driver smoothly elevated the sleek, silver car from the bustling rooftop parking lot, its aerodynamic design reflecting the vibrant city lights as it gracefully drifted into the orderly procession of vehicles gliding above the packed sports arena. Counselor Folly, positioned assertively on the balcony of his luxurious skybox, surveyed the scene above. His sharp gaze followed the high-tech vehicles as they soared into the twilight sky, a sense of urgency brewing within him. "Contact Edward immediately and let him know that trouble is closing in," he instructed, his voice steady and commanding, echoing the gravity of the situation.

"As you wish," one of Counselor Folly's diligent assistants replied, quickly tapping on a sleek communication device to relay the critical message with precision.

"Have my limo driver meet us on the rooftop in five minutes," the Counselor instructed his assistant, his gaze lingering as Jonah's sleek flying car vanished into the horizon. "These chess matches have become dreadfully dull," he continued, tapping his fingers of all four hands impatiently on the polished surface of the rail. "I need to get to my office uptown and devise a strategy to keep this Anderson character away from my operations on the islands." The weight of his words hung in the air, a reminder of the intricate web of power and influence he sought to maintain.

CHAPTER TWO

RETURN TO THE SEWER DISTRICT

0930 HOURS
PRESENT-DAY
THE CHURCH, THE SEWER DISTRICT

The elevator shudders to a halt within the dimly lit confines of the church, its doors creaking open to reveal the imposing figures of two guards stationed just outside. Their stern expressions stand in sharp contrast to the stained-glass windows' solemn beauty, casting colorful patterns on the stone floor. "Welcome, Mr. Anderson," one of the guards intones, his voice deep and authoritative. Doyle meets their gaze, a hint of determination in his eyes. "Good morning," he replies warmly, stepping into the sacred space and feeling the old church's warmth.

"This way, Mr. Anderson," one of the guards announces, his voice echoing off the stone walls as they guide Doyle toward the heavy church doors. With a resolute push, they swing the massive doors open, releasing a gust of cold, wet air that rushes inside. The hinges groan in protest as a sharp, invigorating chill stings Doyle's cheeks, blending with the unmistakable scent of rain-soaked stone.

Stepping outside, he is instantly assaulted by the relentless drumming of rain against his coat, each drop a fleeting sensation of coldness that gradually saturates him. The air is thick and heavy, filled with the earthy aroma of damp soil and the musky scent of refuse, lingering in the narrow alleyways of the Sewer District. The downpour not only numbs his hands and face but also sets an oppressive mood as he braves the elements.

"Doyle! Over here!" a familiar voice calls out, cutting through the sound of steady raindrops hitting the pavement. Doyle squints into the misty drizzle and sees The Driver standing beside a sleek black Volkswagen van, its polished exterior reflecting the muted glow of the streetlights, creating a stunning contrast against the damp, dimly lit surroundings.

"You got her repaired, huh?" Doyle asks, his voice filled with a mix of surprise and admiration as he approaches.

The Driver's face breaks into a broad smile. "This isn't just repaired; it's one of the newly rebuilt models that Deborah had delivered to me today. It's practically brand new."

"Nice. At least Deborah kept her word," Doyle replies, feeling a sense of relief wash over him.

"She always does," The Driver assures him, his tone confident. "Now, climb in before we both get soaked to the bone," he says, gesturing towards the open passenger door, where warm, inviting light spills out into the chilly rain.

"Welcome back to the Sewer District, Doyle. How are you holding up?" The Driver asked, his voice cutting through the rhythmic patter of rain drumming against the van's roof.

"I'm good. I can't complain," Doyle replied, shifting slightly in his seat.

The Driver revved the engine and maneuvered the van away from the curb, the tires splashing through puddles as they hit the slick asphalt. The city lights of the Lower District blurred together in vibrant bursts of color, almost blinding in the relentless downpour. As the van merged onto the main highway, several sleek flying drones zipped by overhead, their buzzing propellers competing with the downpour.

"So, I heard a flying disk crashed on one of the drug islands," The Driver said, glancing sideways at Doyle with curiosity.

Doyle turned to meet his gaze. "That's correct. I'm here to meet with the Warden, Deborah. We need to put a team together to search for the crash site," he explained, his expression serious.

"The brief I received mentioned that," The Driver replied, a playful smirk dancing at the corners of his mouth, hinting at the camaraderie shared between them.

"Don't start that again," Doyle responded with a mock exasperation, rolling his eyes dramatically, although a reluctant smile crept across his face, softening the moment.

The air filled with laughter as The Driver turned back to Doyle, his expression turning thoughtful. "I'm not entirely sure who Deborah will assemble for this team, but I can guarantee there's one person who will definitely be on it."

"Yeah? Who's that?" Doyle asked, curiosity piqued.

"Good morning, Doyle," Eddie the drone chimed in, zipping up from behind the plush back seat of the van with a small whirl of propellers and a friendly gleam in his electronic eyes.

"Eddie!" Doyle exclaimed, his face lighting up with genuine delight. "It's great to see you again!"

"Same to you, sir," Eddie replied, his mechanical voice, infused with a warm, reassuring tone, echoing slightly in the van's confined space. "I'm programmed to accompany you anytime you are in the Sewer District, ensuring you have all the support and protection you need right at your side."

"That's good to know, Eddie," Doyle said, his gaze fixed on the chaotic dance of vehicles maneuvering through the bustling traffic ahead. As he turned to The Driver, a friendly smile crept onto his face. "So, are we not zip-lining to the courthouse today?"

The Driver chuckled, a deep and hearty sound that filled the air. "Nope. Not this time. We're going in through the front door this morning."

"That is equally good to know," Doyle replied, a hint of anticipation in his voice.

The Driver expertly navigated the van into the right lane, and the vehicle smoothly transitioned onto the first bridge in the Sewer District, which arched gracefully toward the Capital Zone. Below them, the river's calm waters glistened in the city lights, creating a stunning contrast to the bustling city above. The sight was comforting to Doyle, who had only ever crossed this river in this direction, suspended hundreds of feet above on a daunting cable. The serenity of the river below was a stark reminder of the thrill and danger that often accompanied their missions.

The Driver navigates towards a fortified gate, where he flashes his badge at a sleek card reader mounted on the side. With a mechanical whir, the gate swings open, granting him access. He maneuvers the vehicle around to the side parking lot, the very spot where he and Doyle had bravely repelled their assailants just a few weeks prior. As the engine comes to a stop, both men step out of the van while Eddie, the vigilant drone, remains stationed in the back seat, keeping a watchful eye on their surroundings.

Instead of making their way to the fire poles usually used for quick ascents, they choose to head toward the main lobby. Upon reaching the grand entrance, they pause before the imposing double doors that lead to the lavish golden elevators. The lobby unfolds before them as a bustling hive of activity, with clusters of people engaged in animated conversations, rushing from one point to another, and the sound of heels clicking against the polished marble floor echoing through the expansive space.

"We're heading to the Mayor's office to meet with both him and the lead attorney this time," The Driver said, his voice steady as they stepped into the elevator. The metal doors slid shut with a dull thud, and the faint hum of machinery filled the air.

Doyle furrowed his brow, a flicker of confusion crossing his face. "Why do we have to meet with the Mayor again?" he asked, glancing at the illuminated floor numbers ticking upward.

The Driver leaned against the elevator wall, his expression thoughtful. "Everything in the Sewer District flows through the Mayor and the Warden. Now that you're a bounty hunter, you are technically under the authority of both the Mayor and the Warden. Jonah may assign you missions from time to time, but remember, you are part of the Sewer District's official authority. Doyle, you are no longer assigned to The Patriot's Group."

The weight of the Driver's words hung in the air, a reminder of the complex web of power in this shadowy world.

The elevator came to a smooth stop, and the doors slowly glided open, revealing an opulent hallway bathed in soft, filtered light. As the two men stepped out, their footsteps echoed against the polished marble floor. Doyle's attention was immediately drawn to the sprawling portraits that decorated the walls, each framed in ornate gold. The images depicted a rugged man dressed in worn hunting attire, confidently standing beside a magnificent dragon, bound in heavy chains. The creature's luminous scales shimmered faintly, and a steel bracket encircled its formidable jaws, offering a stark contrast to the beast's wild beauty. The atmosphere was charged with history and adventure, leaving Doyle both intrigued and awestruck.

The Driver gestured for Doyle to follow him into the main office at the end of the dimly lit hallway. "This way, Doyle," he said, raising his right arm in a welcoming motion while gently guiding him with his left hand on his back, leading him through the polished wooden door and into the office.

Inside, an AI attorney, its sleek frame and sharp features rising to greet them as they entered the Mayor's office. "Welcome, gentlemen. It's wonderful to see you both again," he said, his digital voice resonating with warmth and familiarity.

The Driver and Doyle took their seats beside the attorney, facing the Mayor, who sat behind a grand oak desk, cluttered with papers yet exuding an air of authority. "Good morning," the Mayor said, his tone professional yet cordial.

"Good morning," both men replied in unison, a hint of anticipation threading through their voices as they settled into the distinguished atmosphere of the room.

The Mayor leaned back in his ornate leather chair, a look of deep concern etched across his face. "The details surrounding the crash of that flying disk are exceedingly troubling," he said, sifting through several pages of documents in his hands. "I am convinced this incident is an act of retribution for our decision to destroy the tunnel leading to Dr. Furcus's island."

The attorney, visibly anxious, attempted to interject. "For the record, the court opposed the operation, as I tried to make clear," he began, but the Mayor cut him off sharply.

"I have no interest in your legal justifications. You are programmed solely to safeguard the Sewer District and lack the comprehension necessary to perceive the wider implications of your actions," the Mayor retorted, his voice rising with frustration.

The AI attorney nodded, accepting the critique. "Yes, sir. I understand."

The Mayor then placed the documents carefully on his polished desk and turned to Doyle, his tone shifting to one of gravity. "My last bounty hunter vanished without a trace on one of the islands under the control of Counselor Folly and his gang. One might expect that, given their proximity to Atlantis, these islands would be the safest in the entire Atlantis chain. However, that is far from the truth. The rampant drug trade has infested these islands, making them far more perilous than they appear."

"Mayor, I'm eager to hear any advice you might have on how to proceed with the search for the crash site," Doyle said, his voice steady but filled with urgency.

The Mayor leaned forward, his left arm resting on the desk and his fingers rhythmically tapping against his cheek as he contemplated their next move. "Edward, the eldest son of Counselor Folly, is the de facto ruler of this island, and I'm certain he is anxiously awaiting our search team's arrival. Given the critical nature of this situation, he must become our primary target. Although he has a bounty on him, my initial plan was to navigate through his hierarchy, building rapport and gathering intelligence, rather than starting at the top and risking chaos."

The AI attorney addressed the situation with a calm tone, stating, "Currently, there is no valid warrant for Edward's arrest. The court must uphold the integrity of the law and ensure that no unlawful actions are taken to detain him without just cause."

The Mayor listened intently and pressed further as the attorney continued, "It is important to understand that the Senate will not review the case against Edward for at least one week. Therefore, we cannot issue the necessary warrant for his arrest at this time."

"The Fifth Amendment of Atlantis' constitution grants this court, along with the Warden, the authority to issue arrest warrants for any individual suspected of trafficking drugs or persons to or from Atlantis," the Mayor declared firmly. "Additionally, the amendment specifies that if such a suspect has a documented history of criminal convictions, the court is not required to present the warrant to the Senate for approval beforehand."

"Your Honor, I believe that Counselor Folley will meticulously search for any loopholes in the legal system to secure his son's freedom from prison. The absence of Senate approval could create a significant vulnerability, potentially allowing Edward to slip away from the grasp of justice," the attorney declared, his voice laced with urgency.

The Mayor, poised and resolute, regarded the attorney with seriousness. "I appreciate your thoughtful argument and the weight of your concerns," he said, with a measured tone. "However, I must ultimately deny your request. Therefore, I shall proceed with issuing a warrant for Edward's arrest without further delay."

"As you wish. I will retrieve the warrant for you to sign," the attorney said with a determined nod as he rose from his chair and made his way toward the door, a briefcase in hand.

"Very well," the Mayor replied, watching intently as the attorney exited the room, the clicking of his polished shoes echoing down the corridor. “Those damn attorneys! Sometimes, I can’t shake the feeling that they work for the enemy.”

Doyle chuckled softly and raised an eyebrow in surprise. “I didn’t expect to encounter this level of politics in Atlantis, especially given its enchanting, otherworldly nature.”

The Mayor leaned back in his chair, the leather creaking under his weight, and let out a contemplative sigh. “It’s not as rampant as it is in the known world,” he said, his gaze drifting to the intricate patterns of the ceiling, “but it certainly lingers just below the surface, like a hidden current in a crystal-clear stream.” A flicker of frustration crossed his face, revealing the strain of his responsibilities. “The real issue lies with the AI’s programming. The developers relied on legal cases from the known world. As a result, the AI sometimes reflects rather corrupt ideas and biases,” he explained, shaking his head slowly as if trying to dispel the troubling thoughts. “We must also remember that the hybrids who programmed the AI are part fallen angel; they do not always have humanity’s best interests in mind.”

“I can definitely see how that would lead to complications,” Doyle replied, his expression thoughtful.

At that moment, the AI attorney entered the room, his mechanical demeanor sharp and efficient. “Here it is, Mayor,” he said, presenting the warrant with an elegant flourish as he laid it on the polished oak desk.

“Very good, thank you,” the Mayor replied, a note of approval in his voice. “You are dismissed.”

With a courteous bow of his head, the AI attorney retreated from the office, his footsteps echoing softly along the marble hallway as he disappeared around the corner, leaving the three men to ponder the complexities of their world.

The Mayor fixed his gaze on The Driver and Doyle, his expression serious. "I'm dispatching one of my most skilled jungle trackers to accompany you on this mission. He has a unique heritage: his father is a revered Comanche war chief, and his mother is of mixed blood, making him one-quarter hybrid. This background gives him an intimate understanding of the islands' terrain and wildlife, and the expertise to navigate their complexities. His name is Sonny. He does not speak much, but you'll be happy to have him on the team."

The men sat in silence for a few minutes before the Mayor spoke, "You need to know, as you prepare to embark on your journey, be forewarned: the waters surrounding this archipelago are notoriously perilous. They teem with fearsome Krakens, colossal sea monsters rumored to drag entire ships to the depths, as well as treacherous reefs that could spell disaster for even the most seasoned sailors who venture unprepared."

"Kraken? You mean like the legendary sea monster that sailors speak of in hushed tones?" asked Doyle, his eyes wide with both excitement and trepidation.

The Mayor let out a hearty laugh, his voice booming across the office. "Yes, exactly like that, Doyle! But worry not; we have designed an exceptional ship equipped to navigate these dangerous waters safely. We modeled it after the most famous pirate vessel in history, Queen Anne's Revenge, notorious for her speed and ferocity."

"Blackbeard's ship?" Doyle exclaimed, his intrigue deepening.

"That's correct!" the Mayor exclaimed, his voice filled with enthusiasm. "However, unlike the infamous vessel that met its tragic end in the treacherous shallows, this ship is meticulously designed to navigate the seas safely and avoid such disasters. You can set sail with complete confidence," he added, a proud smile illuminating his face. "With that said, gentlemen, I wish you every success in executing the arrest warrant for Edward and in your safe return to the splendid city of Atlantis."

The three men exchanged firm handshakes, a silent pact forged between them, before The Driver and Doyle stepped out of the office. They made their way toward the polished elevators, their footsteps echoing in the spacious corridor as anticipation thrummed in the air.

Doyle turned to The Driver as they stepped into the elevator, a mix of curiosity and disbelief in his eyes. "A year ago, I never would have imagined a world inhabited by hybrids, four-armed beings, dragons soaring through the skies, and krakens lurking beneath the waves. What other bizarre mysteries could await me?"

With a knowing smile, The Driver leaned slightly closer and replied, "You wouldn't believe me if I told you."

"That's exactly what I'm afraid of," Doyle admitted, his voice tinged with unease, as the elevator doors creaked open slowly.

Standing a few feet away was a striking figure, a man clad in a vibrant orange three-piece suit that contrasted sharply with his pale green skin. His attire was further accentuated by a sharply tailored black fedora perched atop his head, and his face was framed by three intense, fiery-red eyes that seemed to pierce the corridor's dim light. He approached Doyle and The Driver with a confident stride.

Doyle looked up, a mix of astonishment and apprehension crossing his features. "Who in the hell is that?" he asked, gesturing toward the unusual man.

"That is Augustine," The Driver explained calmly, his tone reflecting a deep familiarity. "He's the leader of the MIA gang here in the Sewer District, another one of the Counselor's sons. His reputation precedes him, so tread carefully."

"Well, well, well. If it isn't the military boy," Augustine said, his voice dripping with sarcasm as he sauntered up to Doyle, invading his personal space with an air of arrogance.

"Which eye should I look at? The one in the middle?" Doyle shot back, a cocky grin spreading across his face. He lifted his arm, placing his hand firmly on Augustine's chest, using his thick forearm to push him back with an unexpected force.

Augustine stumbled backward, his expression shifting from smugness to indignation as four of his henchmen rushed to his side, muscles tense and ready for confrontation. "You keep your hands off me, Army boy!" he snapped, anger flaring in his voice like a wildfire.

Doyle stepped forward again, his stance wide and unyielding. "Then you keep your foul-smelling breath out of my face, unless you want me to rearrange your features," he retorted, his tone carrying the weight of a simmering threat.

"How dare you threaten me! Do you know who I am?" Augustine raged, his eyes narrowing dangerously. "I'm a god here in the Sewer

District!" His voice rose, echoing off the grimy, graffiti-covered walls that surrounded them.

Just then, a dozen AI police officers arrived on the scene, their sleek uniforms shining under the flickering light of a nearby streetlamp. Augustine, flanked by his imposing bodyguards, straightened his tie with a haughty air. "I know who you are, Doyle Anderson. You are the Army hero responsible for obliterating the tunnel to Dr. Furcus's island. You are a criminal, and I intend to bring you to justice," he declared, his tone oozing with authority as he squared his shoulders against the encroaching tension."

The Driver strolled over to Doyle, the tension in the air thick as he spoke with a calm yet authoritative tone, "Just ignore him. He's just like his father, always craving attention and eager to create a scene."

Augustine, with a sharp glint of disdain in his eyes, turned his gaze to The Driver and remarked, "Another hybrid gone rogue, aligning himself with the feeble human race."

Doyle, feeling the sting of the insult, shot back defiantly, "Feeble? I just pushed you away using only one hand!"

"I wasn't prepared; you played dirty," Augustine retorted, his frustration evident in his clenched fists.

"Come on, Doyle, let it go," The Driver urged again, his voice steady, trying to diffuse the simmering tension between them.

"Hang on a second," Doyle replied, making his way over to Augustine with a curious look. "What's the story behind your green skin and those three eyes? Is it an unfortunate accident, or do you just neglect your appearance?" Doyle asked, a playful smile creeping across his face.

In response, Augustine lunged forward, a flash of frustration in his expression. However, Doyle was quick on his feet; he sidestepped deftly, managing to knock the hat off Augustine's head with a swift motion. The sudden scuffle drew the AI policemen's attention, who surged forward to intervene, creating a barrier between the two men. Meanwhile, The Driver expertly navigated the chaos, guiding Doyle determinedly toward the exit and ensuring he avoided any further confrontation.

"I'll get you, Army boy!" shouted Augustine, his voice echoing ominously as he glared at the towering AI policemen standing guard.

Doyle grinned defiantly, shouting back, "I'm looking forward to it!" He stepped outside, his heart racing with adrenaline, accompanied by The Driver.

Turning to Doyle, The Driver arched an eyebrow, curiosity etched on his face. "What's gotten into you today, Doyle? You seem… different."

"I can't quite put my finger on it," Doyle admitted, a sense of exhilaration coursing through him. "I haven't felt this vibrant in years. It's as if I'm regaining a strength I thought I'd lost two decades ago."

The Driver nodded, his expression becoming serious. "No doubt that the Counselor sent Augustine to antagonize you. That's their usual tactic, provoking people to incite chaos. I can only imagine how Deborah will react to this. I'm sure she'll make her feelings known to Counselor Folly without hesitation."

"I'm used to having to deal with those types of people, or I guess now, hybrids," Doyle said, laughing.

"Just get in the van, we need to go meet with Deborah," The Driver told him as he walked to the van.

Eddie, the drone, came to life as soon as Doyle entered the van, "I forgot to tell you to wear your earpiece, Doyle. I saw Augustine enter the courthouse looking for you."

"Yeah, that's on me, Eddie. I forgot too," Doyle replied, reaching back and taking the earpiece from Eddie and placing it in his ear.

The Driver inserted the key into the ignition, and the van's engine roared to life with a deep, throaty rumble as they eased out of the dimly lit parking lot. The glow of the streetlights lit their path as they wound through the streets toward the vibrant façade of the Grand Theatre, adorned with dazzling neon and posters announcing the latest performances. He glanced at Doyle and said, "Deborah is currently captivating the audience in her role as Miss Candy. Let's head there and follow her to the Warden's office afterward."

Doyle nodded, a determined glint in his eyes. "Sounds like a solid plan to me."

Back inside the courthouse, Augustine was inciting a whirlwind of discontent. His voice rose powerfully, echoing like a battle cry off the high ceilings and polished marble walls. "That guy is only here in the Sewer District to strip away the few freedoms we have left!" he exclaimed, his voice filled with fervor. "I urge everyone to rise up, take to the streets, and protest against the idea of him and Deborah becoming the new Warden!" Just as his impassioned words reached a crescendo, four robotic AI policemen surged forward, overpowering him and pushing him through the heavy double doors of the courthouse lobby, unceremoniously casting him out into the relentless rain.

CHAPTER THREE

THE DREAM TEAM

1730 HOURS
PRESENT-DAY
THE GRAND THEATRE, THE SEWER DISTRICT

The atmosphere inside the Grand Theatre was electric with anticipation as the lights illuminated the stage, showcasing the stunning figure of Miss Candy. The audience erupted into enthusiastic cheers, drowning out all sound as Doyle leaned towards The Driver, admiration gleaming in his eyes. "She looks absolutely breathtaking today," he remarked, his voice barely audible above the clamor.

"She truly does," The Driver replied, his gaze fixed intently on the stage.

Before them, Miss Candy, adorned in alluring black lingerie, sat provocatively on the edge of a grand, plush bed that seemed to envelop her in its opulent fabric. Tension filled the air as a man, desperation etched on his face, implored her not to end their tumultuous relationship. In a fit of fury, he lunged forward, his hands reaching out in a moment of violent desperation, and shouted, "If I can't have you, no one will!"

Miss Candy struggled against his grip, her elegant features contorting with both defiance and fear. But just as quickly as the struggle began, her body went limp, as if surrendering to the weight of the emotional turmoil. The scene climaxed, and the curtains closed, wrapping the audience in a thick blanket of silence after the drama storm they had just witnessed.

The crowd erupted into chaos, hurling cups and crumpled popcorn bags at the heavy curtains on stage. "Miss Candy can't be dead!" a voice pierced through the tumult, filled with disbelief and anger. Amidst the commotion, The Driver and Doyle deftly maneuvered through the frenzied audience, making their way down the dimly lit back hallway that led to Miss Candy's dressing room.

As they approached the door, a burly guard with a stern expression stepped into their path, arms crossed defiantly.

"You two are not allowed here," he barked, his voice firm and uncompromising.

Unfazed, The Driver calmly produced his badge, holding it up for the guard to see. "We're here to see Miss Candy," he stated with authority.

The guard scrutinized the badge for a moment, his steely gaze shifting from the identification to The Driver's face. Finally, with a reluctant nod, he relented, "Very well, sir."

The Driver confidently approached the door, his footsteps firm against the polished floor, and knocked briskly on Miss Candy's dressing room door. "Miss Candy, it's The Driver and Doyle," he announced, his voice steady and authoritative.

"Come in!" Miss Candy called with a lively tone, the sound reverberating off the walls.

With a swift motion, The Driver pushed the door open, allowing a sliver of light to spill into the dim room as he and Doyle stepped inside. The atmosphere shifted instantly as Miss Candy turned to them, her long silk housecoat falling open, revealing her ample figure in all its glory. The sight was stunning, her large breasts and bare skin illuminated in the soft light, creating an almost ethereal presence.

"Holy moly!" Doyle exclaimed, his eyes widening in shock as he quickly looked away, a rush of crimson flooding his cheeks and betraying his embarrassment.

"What's wrong, darling?" Miss Candy asked.

Avoiding her gaze, Doyle responded, "We are here to see Deborah, not you as Miss Candy."

Miss Candy adjusted her housecoat, its fabric soft against her skin, put on her eyeglasses, and looked at Doyle with a mischievous glint in her eye. "Very well, but mark my words, Doyle: one day, you and I, in the persona of Miss Candy, are going to spend some unforgettable time together."

Doyle chuckled lightly, shaking his head. "Don't hold your breath, Miss Candy. As I have told you countless times before, I'm happily married and quite content with my life as it is," he replied, a hint of exasperation in his tone.

With a playful smile, Miss Candy stepped behind an intricately designed dressing wall, her silhouette vanishing for a moment. "Ah, but Miss Candy is quite tenacious and will not give up until she has you in her grasp. Deborah, on the other hand," she continued, stepping back into sight, now fully embodying the demure and elegant character of Deborah, "will always honor your wishes."

She walked over to a modest bar nestled in the corner of the dimly lit room and poured three drinks, the amber liquid catching the low light. "I've been briefed about the flying disk that crashed on one of the notorious drug islands," she said, her tone infused with both concern and curiosity.

Doyle nodded in agreement, his expression serious. "That's correct. I need your expertise, along with that of our small team, to pinpoint the crash site. We hope to locate the officers and bring them back safely."

Deborah set her glass down and turned to face him squarely. "I trust the mayor has informed you about who governs this island?"

Doyle replied, "Yes. His name is Edward."

Deborah took a deliberate sip of her drink, her eyes narrowing slightly. "Edward is my ex-husband and the father of my son."

Doyle furrowed his brow as he processed this revelation. "That's how the mayor explained it to me," he said, taking a moment to gauge her reaction. "Was he Miss Candy's husband or Deborah's?"

Deborah laughed. "Miss Candy would have nothing to do with him. I married him as Deborah. I created Miss Candy and the Bartender to help me forget that part of my life."

Screams pierced the air outside the dressing room door, a cacophony of disbelief and outrage. "Miss Candy cannot be dead!" one voice rang out, filled with anguish.

"I don't think they were pleased with the way the play concluded," The Driver noted dryly, watching the commotion unfold.

With a steadying breath, Deborah strode to the door and swung it open, revealing a throng of anxious faces. "Everyone will have to wait until the new play starts in a few weeks to discover if she survived," she declared, her tone calm but authoritative.

"Who are you? Where is Miss Candy?" a man demanded fiercely, his frustration palpable.

"She has already left the building," Deborah replied crisply, offering no further explanation as she gently closed the door, cutting off the whirlwind of panic outside.

"They don't realize that you're Miss Candy?" Doyle asked, raising an eyebrow in surprise.

"They don't," Deborah replied, a hint of amusement in her voice.

"Come in, Doyle," Eddie's voice crackled through the earpiece, urgent and clear.

"Go ahead, Eddie," Doyle responded, his expression shifting to one of concern.

"Doyle, we have a serious situation on our hands," Eddie explained, his tone heavy with gravity.

Doyle glanced at The Driver, who remained stoic and watchful, before turning to Deborah, whose confidence seemed to radiate even in the tense atmosphere. "What's the problem, Eddie?" he asked, his curiosity piqued.

"Augustine has just arrived with six members of his MIA gang," Eddie warned, the weight of his words hanging in the air. "They're armed, and we can't underestimate what they're capable of."

"I hear you, Eddie," Doyle replied.

"Doyle," Eddie said, his voice laced with urgency, "Augustine is now telling people streaming out of the Grand Theatre that it was your idea to kill off Miss Candy in the play."

Deborah turned to Doyle with a determined look in her eyes. "You will exit the theatre with me from the rooftop," she stated firmly, before shifting her gaze to The Driver. "Can you maneuver your van around to the back exit?"

A shadow of concern crossed The Driver's face as he processed the situation. "Eddie is in the van," he replied, his voice steady but laced with urgency.

"Is there any way we can get Eddie to find a good hiding spot inside while you program the van to maneuver to the back exit?" Deborah inquired, her brow furrowing with worry as she thought through the plan.

The Driver nodded, regaining his confidence. "He knows how to stay out of sight. We can handle it."

With a quick nod of acknowledgment, Deborah continued, "You meet Eddie at the van, and then head to the church. Doyle and I, along with Sonny, will rendezvous with you there after we go over the plans in my office in the Warden's block."

"Eddie," Doyle instructed, his tone steady and confident, "Stay out of sight inside the van as The Driver navigates it around to the back entrance. The Driver will be waiting for you."

"I'm on it," Eddie responded, his voice filled with determination as he prepared to execute the task.

The Driver strode over to a large, ornate carpet suspended from the wall. With a firm grip, he pulled it aside, revealing a hidden door, an escape route he and Doyle had used weeks earlier. "I will meet you both at the church," he said with a mysterious glance before disappearing into the shadowy space beyond the door, leaving a palpable tension in the air.

"Follow me, Doyle," Deborah commanded, her voice steady as she made her way to the bar, an unassuming piece of furniture now buzzing with secrets. She pressed a concealed button beneath the counter, and with a soft whir, a small panel in the ceiling slid open, allowing a sturdy ladder to lower with a smooth, almost theatrical grace.

Doyle watched with keen interest, his heart racing. "I hope there are no zip lines in our near future," he joked, trying to lighten the mood.

Deborah responded with a quick, determined smirk as she retrieved a small pistol, its metal gleaming in the low light, and tucked it securely into the back of her pants. "No zip lines. We are heading to my flying motorcycle," she declared, her eyes sparkling with excitement and a hint of adventure.

"Flying motorcycle?" Doyle echoed, a mix of surprise and intrigue in his voice. The idea seemed both thrilling and surreal, promising a journey unlike anything he had ever encountered.

Deborah approached the sturdy metal ladder, her heart racing with anticipation as she began to climb. "Don't look too hard at my butt, Doyle. I'm not wearing panties," she called over her shoulder, a playful smile dancing on her lips.

"I'm not even going to dignify that with a response," Doyle said, his voice laced with playful annoyance.

Deborah chuckled, the sound bright and cheerful. "You're just too easy," she teased. Once she reached the top, she glanced back down towards him, a mischievous glint in her eyes. "Hurry up, and I'll close it up!"

With determination, Doyle climbed the ladder and stepped into the attic-like room, a treasure trove of Miss Candy's whimsical creations. The dim light revealed countless outfits draped over mannequins, their hollow forms casting strange shadows that added an eerie ambiance to the space. Each ensemble glittered with vibrant colors and intricate designs, hinting at stories long forgotten.

Deborah, feeling the thrill of their secret venture, reached for a button on the opposite wall. With a press, the ladder retracted silently, and the ceiling sealed shut, leaving them in a cozy realm of fabric and memories.

"Doyle, The Driver, and I are in the van and clear of the area," Eddie, the drone, said through Doyle's earpiece.

"That is good to hear. We will see you soon," replied Doyle.

"Follow me, Doyle," Deborah instructed, gesturing toward the far end of the vast storage room. Her footsteps echoed softly against the hardwood floor, a rhythmic backdrop to the intriguing chaos around them. Doyle fell into step behind her, his eyes darting over the eclectic array of brightly colored outfits that adorned the metallic racks, each one more striking than the last.

He noticed scattered components of half-assembled AI robots, gleaming metal limbs, intricate circuit boards, and clusters of wires sprawled across the floor like a tangled web. The air was thick with the scent of oil and the faint buzz of machinery, creating an atmosphere at once industrial and alive. Doyle couldn't help but wonder about the purpose of this unconventional space. "What is this place used for?" he asked, a mix of wonder and curiosity evident in his voice, eager to uncover the secrets hidden within the clutter.

"I use this space primarily to store my collection of old outfits, each one a vibrant relic from past performances, and, in addition, to design and construct intricate AI robots for my theatrical productions. Training these robots is a breeze compared to managing human performers; they seamlessly adapt to my artistic vision. In fact, during most of my plays, I find myself the sole figure on stage, the only one with real blood coursing through my veins," Deborah said, a spark of pride lighting up her features. She halted before a pair of imposing double doors, the rich wood grain glimmering in the warm light of the room. With a sudden, authoritative motion, she flung both doors open, revealing an unexpected sight: two sets of sleek, polished fire poles that gleamed with promise.

Doyle's expression shifted to one of annoyance. "Not again. Do you people never use stairs or elevators?" he exclaimed, the frustration bubbling in his voice.

"They're simply too slow for what we need," Deborah replied, her tone unfazed as she confidently stepped onto one of the small, round disks positioned around the fire pole, the metal cool beneath her feet. "What are you waiting for?" she challenged him, her eyes fixed on him with a mix of urgency and encouragement.

With a heavy sigh, Doyle stepped onto the second disk, his palms wrapping around the smooth surface of the pole. In an exhilarating instant, the disk catapulted him upward, the room below blurring into a dizzying rush as he soared more than twenty stories into the darkness, leaving behind the ordinary and venturing toward the exhilarating unknown of the rooftop.

Doyle steps off the shimmering disk and into a dark rooftop room, its expansive windows overlooking the bustling city below. The sudden change in height overwhelms him, and he grasps a sturdy metal handrail to steady himself as a wave of dizziness washes over him. Just behind him, Deborah emerges, her footsteps soft against the polished floor. She immediately senses his disorientation and quickly moves to his side, wrapping her arms around him for support. "Take a few deep breaths, Doyle," she encourages gently, her voice calm and reassuring.

"I'll be okay," Doyle replies, trying to shake off the disorientation as he gently pulls away from her embrace, determined to regain his composure in the vibrant, open space.

The rooftop room exuded an air of isolation, its bare walls echoing the silence, with only a striking piece of equipment breaking the monotony just a few steps away. It resembled a motorcycle without wheels, elegantly hovering a few inches above the polished wooden floor, as if suspended by an invisible force. The design was sleek and aerodynamic, with handlebars that gracefully arch back toward the rear, hinting at a future filled with speed and adventure.

The leather seat, a rich, deep mahogany, was not only inviting but also intricately crafted, featuring ergonomic indentations that suggested comfort for two riders. Each contour whispered of countless journeys yet to be taken, while the leather's subtle sheen reflected the soft ambient light streaming through the skylights above, enhancing the machine's allure. The room, drenched in a warm glow, held an enticing promise of exploration and the thrill of the unknown, as if calling out to those daring enough to seize the adventure ahead.

Doyle rubbed his stubbled chin as he regained his balance, allowing the thrum of the flying motorcycle beneath him to settle. "That's a striking bike you've got there. I didn't think they allowed flying vehicles in The Sewer District," he observed, arching an eyebrow.

"They don't," Deborah replied with a confident grin. "But I'm not your ordinary prisoner, either."

"Clearly," Doyle replied, a smirk spreading across his face as he took in her defiant demeanor.

With an air of playful rebellion, Deborah strode over to the sleek machine and expertly swung her leg over the seat, settling into position. "Saddle up, cowboy," she called over her shoulder, her eyes sparkling with mischief.

Doyle rolled his eyes, a mix of amusement and apprehension flaring within him. He approached the motorcycle, maneuvered his leg over with care, and sank into the contoured seat designed for speed. "Just don't throw me off this thing," he said, half-joking, but the tension in his voice betrayed his uncertainty.

Deborah laughed, a bright sound that cut through the air. "I promise, there's zero chance I'd ever lose you, darling," she teased. Her expression shifted slightly, taking on a more serious tone. "Now, please fasten your seatbelt. We might need to pull some sharp maneuvers to navigate through to the Warden's block."

The engine hummed to life beneath them, ready to transport them into the chaotic skies of The Sewer District.

Deborah reached into a side pocket of her gear and retrieved two pairs of sleek goggles, their lenses glinting in the dim light. She handed one pair to Doyle, her expression serious yet playful. "You'll want these on; the relentless downpour outside will make visibility nearly impossible."

Doyle grasped the goggles and nodded, a hint of excitement in his voice. "Got it, thanks," he said as he settled the goggles snugly over his eyes, the world outside shifting into a blurred haze.

"Now, feel free to hold on to me tightly if you need to," Deborah teased, her eyes sparkling with humor.

Doyle glanced over the sides of the formidable motorcycle and noted the sturdy handholds designed for passengers. “Thanks, but I think I’ll just stick with the bars,” he said, a smirk forming on his lips.

“If those grip bars start to pinch your hands, just remember that mine are much softer and warmer,” she replied with a light-hearted laugh that echoed in the cramped space.

“Geez,” Doyle said, shaking his head in mock disbelief, a smile tugging at the corners of his mouth.

Just then, the far wall of their dimly lit sanctuary slid open with a mechanical hum, revealing the stormy skies beyond. Deborah’s fingers danced over the throttle, igniting the engine’s roar. With a surge of power, the flying motorcycle shot out of the rooftop room, launching them into the turbulent, rain-soaked sky, where droplets cascaded like glistening pearls around them.

“It will only take us a few minutes to reach my warden’s office,” Deborah said, her voice steady despite the chaos around them. “It’s suspended from the ceiling of The Sewer District, directly above the prison.” As she spoke, her sharp eyes caught sight of four small drones swooping in from the shadows, their metallic bodies glinting ominously in the dim light. “Hang on, Doyle. Drones usually don’t fly this high. There are four of them, and they’re gaining on us quickly; must be the MIA gang’s doing.”

With a practiced motion, she reached back and pulled a compact pistol from the waistband of her pants. The first drone zipped past her head with a high-pitched whine, narrowly missing her. Aiming, she fired a bolt of electricity that struck the drone, causing it to erupt in a shower of sparks before plummeting to the ground.

As she maneuvered the motorcycle, two more drones closed in, buzzing like angry hornets. Deborah pushed the throttle, the engine roaring to life, and executed a daring flip, turning the flying bike upside down. Below them, the ground seemed to rush away, and Doyle's heart raced as he glanced downward just in time to see one of the drones collide with the bike's underside, bursting into flames and sending a plume of smoke trailing behind them. The explosion's heat briefly illuminated the dim street, a stark reminder of the danger they faced as they barreled toward the warden's office.

Deborah expertly righted the flying bike, tilting it back to an upright position as Doyle leaned forward, the wind whipping over his bald head. "My hat flew off while we were upside down!" he shouted, eyes wide with adrenaline.

"I'll replace it, don't worry!" she called back, her voice steady despite the chaos around them. As she glanced at the two remaining drones that hummed ominously beside them, a sudden burst of urgency surged within her. With a quick flick of the wrist, she veered the bike sharply to the left, her move catching one of the drones off guard. It clipped its propellers against the motorcycle and spiraled into a reckless tumble, crashing into one of the towering skyscrapers that defined the Capital Zone.

"Hang on!" she yelled, her heart racing as she plunged downward, navigating swiftly between the imposing Capitol building and a massive parking structure. The last drone, relentless in its pursuit, pursued them with threatening precision, firing shots that zipped past them like angry wasps.

Determined, Deborah ducked beneath the sprawling bridge that connected the Capital Zone to the ominous silhouette of the Prison Zone. With a burst of speed, she shot upward into the vast expanse of the sky, the city sprawling below them like a miniature model.

"Oh shit!" Doyle exclaimed, his voice tinged with exhilaration and fear as the sheer force of their rapid ascent pressed him back against the bike's cushioned backrest, the world around them a blur of colors and shadows.

Deborah released the throttle of her flying motorcycle, allowing the powerful machine to coast to a sudden stop as the last drone chased closely behind. The abrupt halt caught the drone off guard, sending it crashing forcefully into the rear of her bike. In an instant, the impact ignited a fiery explosion, engulfing the drone in flames as it careened uncontrollably toward the river below. Deborah's heart raced as she watched the flaming wreckage plunge into the water, sending a sizzling splash that billowed steam into the air. With a surge of adrenaline, she quickly pressed the throttle again, skillfully stopping the motorcycle's fall away from the river's treacherous embrace.

Deborah expertly piloted the flying bike through the dark sky, its powerful engine humming beneath them as they soared above the formidable prison. The prison lights glinted off the high concrete walls, casting long shadows over the barren grounds below. With a smooth descent, she guided the bike to a gentle landing on the expansive platform of the Warden's Block, her heart racing with exhilaration.

After they touched down, she turned to Doyle, her cheeks flushed with excitement. "That was absolutely thrilling!" she exclaimed, her voice bubbling with enthusiasm.

Doyle, still feeling the rush of adrenaline, wiped the beads of water from his gleaming bald head, a look of mild dread crossing his face. "Let's not do that again, okay?" he replied, his tone a mix of disbelief and relief.

Once the bike was secure, Deborah gracefully dismounted with the poise of a seasoned adventurer. Her clothing was soaked from the rain, revealing her large nipples pushing through her shirt. She then reached out to help Doyle, who reluctantly clambered off and took a moment to gather his bearings. As he peered over the edge, his gaze fixed on the sprawling prison, a labyrinth of steel and concrete that loomed ominously on the horizon.

His attention was suddenly captivated by a majestic dragon, its scales shimmering like molten gold in the dim light, standing sentinel beside a large barn-like structure. "Is that why the prison walls are so tall?" he asked, his voice laced with awe and curiosity.

Deborah nodded, a serious expression clouding her features. "The Sewer District draws high-profile visitors from realms both known and unknown," she explained, gesturing toward the watchful dragon. "Many of our visitors are ill-equipped to grasp the existence of such extraordinary creatures. The height of the walls is merely a precaution, built to guard against those who may underestimate the perilous nature of our world." The dragon, with its fierce gaze, seemed to embody that very warning, a guardian against the untold mysteries that lay within the fortress.

The door to the Warden's office slid open, revealing a man with bluish skin and a large, flat-brimmed hat. "Doyle, this is Sonny, our jungle tracker. He is the son of a Comanche war chief," Deborah explained.

Sonny approached Doyle and extended his hand. "Nice to meet you," he said, then pulled out a slingshot and fired a small rock at the dragon below.

The dragon slowly lifted its head, looking at Sonny as it spoke, "Who casts rocks from his high pulpit?"

CHAPTER FOUR

COUNSELOR FOLLY

1745 HOURS
PRESENT-DAY
THE RESTAURANT DISTRICT, ATLANTIS

The setting sun casts a vibrant golden glow that washes over the skyline as it descends behind the majestic skyscrapers of the upscale Restaurant District. Inside a sophisticated Italian restaurant, the atmosphere buzzes with the lively sounds of clinking glasses and soft conversations, intertwined with the intoxicating aromas of rich marinara sauce, roasted garlic, and fragrant herbs. At the head of the elegantly adorned table, Counselor Folly commands attention. His demeanor is reminiscent of a mafia boss, exuding authority and gravitas that fill the room.

Folly, a man of imposing stature and a carefully groomed appearance, indulges in a perfectly crispy chicken wing, its succulence evident with every bite. Juices run down his chin, but he seems unconcerned, too absorbed in the unfolding conversation. With a casual flick of his wrist, he gestures toward his attentive entourage, leaning forward slightly as he addresses them in a tone that blends casual inquiry with underlying intensity. "Tell me, did the MIA gang take Doyle and Deborah out?" The question lingers in the air, thick with tension and anticipation, as his companions lean in, intrigued by the implications of his words and eager to share in the unfolding drama.

A large, profoundly fat man, his expansive belly spilling over the edge of the chair and straining the seams of his shirt, sat to the right of Folly. He cleared his throat, his voice quivering with unease as he spoke. "Sir, we launched an offensive with four of our drones, but it appears that Deborah outsmarted us; she destroyed all of them and escaped without a trace."

Folly's frustration erupted like a volcano as he slammed all four of his fists onto the polished table, the sound resonating through the room like a thunderclap. "Dammit! They must not be allowed to reach that island in their relentless quest for the flying disk remains. Augustine has always been a disappointment!"

The hefty man, visibly shaken by Folly's outburst, tried to interject, his voice urgent. "Sir, he is not weak. He has managed the MIA gang in The Sewer District with remarkable skill, maintaining order in a chaotic environment…"

Before he could fully articulate his defense, Folly's powerful arm lashed out like a whip, delivering a swift and stinging blow to the man's face. The force of the strike sent the man's dinner plate soaring dramatically through the air, clattering to the ground as he toppled backward from his chair, his eyes wide with shock and confusion. The once lively atmosphere suddenly felt thick with tension, the remaining diners watching in stunned silence.

Folly rose with an air of menace, his silhouette looming over the plump figure of the man sprawled unceremoniously on the cold concrete floor. His eyes narrowed as he glared down, his voice dripping with disdain. "You allowed this so-called Anderson to destroy the tunnel that served as a crucial artery to Dr. Furcus's remote island. That tunnel was not just a passageway; it was the linchpin of our extensive global human trafficking operation, carefully orchestrated over years of meticulous planning. Now, with its destruction, our entire network teeters on the edge of catastrophe. If we let Deborah and Anderson reach this other island and uncover our intricate drug operations hidden within its depths, the very foundation of my organization will shatter like glass, leaving us vulnerable and exposed."

The overweight man lay helplessly on his back, his gaze fixed on Counselor Folly, who loomed over him with an air of unsettling authority. "Yes, sir. I understand," he replied, his voice trembling slightly.

Folly, with a calculated slowness, retrieved a sleek .38 revolver from the depths of his tailored coat. "I don't think you do," he said with a chilling calmness, just before pulling the trigger and sending a bullet strikingly accurate between the fat man's eyes. The echo of the gunshot reverberated in the room, a grim punctuation to the moment.

"Clean up this mess before I return from the bathroom," Folly commanded, his tone laced with menace, as he turned on his heel and strode away, leaving chaos in his wake.

Folly stepped into the expansive bathroom, where the air was thick with warmth and a gentle mist swirled around him, a byproduct of the steam rising from the adjoining steam room. The faint aroma of eucalyptus lingered, mingling with the scent of warm tiles and the sound of dripping water. He approached a separate door to the left, pushing it open to reveal the steam room's inviting fog.

Inside, the atmosphere was almost ethereal, with soft, diffused light illuminating the steam and creating a hazy ambiance. Seated on a polished wooden bench was a figure cloaked in a pristine white towel, casually adjusting its drape. This man, known to many as The Whistler, had an enigmatic air about him, and his fingers played a rhythmic tune as he whistled, the sound echoing softly in the misty enclosure.

Folly took a seat across from him, his posture relaxed yet purposeful. "I have a job for you," he stated, his voice smooth but laced with an underlying urgency.

The Whistler lifted his head, his curious gaze meeting Folly's. A wry smile crested his lips as he replied, "Let me guess. You want me to take care of that Anderson man?"

Folly let out a light, genuine laugh, the sound resonating warmly in the steam-laden air. "You're sharp. That is correct. But there's more to it; I also need Deborah dealt with," he added, his expression shifting to one of seriousness that cut through the cozy steam like a knife.

The Whistler's amusement gradually faded, giving way to an air of deep contemplation. He resumed whistling for a moment, letting the melodic notes dance through the warm, humid air, only for them to fall silent again, creating a palpable tension. "That's not possible. Deborah is off-limits," he declared, his voice shifting to a tone of quiet intensity. The gravity of his words hung heavily between them, thickening the atmosphere with unspoken implications as Folly grappled with the weight of what he had just heard.

Folly, unable to contain his frustration, stomped his foot defiantly. "I say she is not off-limits!" he retorted, his voice firm.

Once again, the Whistler broke into a whistle, this time the notes piercing the silence louder than before, their haunting echoes swirling around Folly's ears like a chilling breeze. "If I remove Deborah," he said, his eyes narrowing, "You will be dead by dawn, along with each one of your children." The warning hung ominously in the air, underscoring the dangerous stakes of their conversation.

"How dare you threaten me! Do you have any idea who you're speaking to?" Folly exclaimed, his voice laced with a seething rage that radiated from his very core.

The Whistler, a figure cloaked in mystery, responded with a sly smile that only deepened the tension in the air. "I haven't threatened you," he said, his tone calm and measured, cutting through his fury like a knife. "I've simply cautioned you that your choices will carry consequences, not from me, of course, but from the very forces that maintain the delicate balance of this world. She has powerful allies now; she has transformed into a woman who truly fears God."

Counselor Folly muttered to himself, his frustration evident as he pounded his four hands rhythmically against the worn wooden bench on which he sat. The deep creases of worry etched into his brow seemed to deepen as he slowly turned to face The Whistler. "Very well," he said, the weight of his words heavy in the air. "You take care of Anderson, and I will handle Deborah."

The Whistler paused, the sweet, lilting notes of his whistling fading into a heavy silence as he locked eyes with Folly. A calculating glint sparkled in his gaze. "Why do you want Deborah removed? She is a crucial figure in maintaining order within The Sewer District, and being confined to that prison, she poses little threat to you."

Folly shifted uneasily on the wooden bench, its surface creaking under the tension of his presence. "She has hidden my grandson in that labyrinthine underground world ever since her divorce from my son."

"The fact that your son, Edward, was a notorious ladies' man means little in this context. He has fathered countless children throughout the unexplored corners of our world," The Whistler explained, the corners of his mouth twitching in amusement.

"That means nothing in this situation!" Folly shouted, his grip tightening around the bench as if he could crush it with his anger.

"I would argue it mattered immensely to Deborah," The Whistler shot back, a hint of challenge in his voice.

Folly slammed one hand against his leg in frustration, pointing accusingly at The Whistler. "She has disrespected my family, and that is utterly unforgivable. Her son, my grandson, will be groomed to work for me in the family business. He has no choice; my will is law. Deborah will bend to my demands, or she will be removed."

The Whistler studied Folly thoughtfully, the ambient steam curling around them like a shroud. "I think you are a fool, but that is your right. A fool knows only what he knows."

Folly rocked back and forth on the bench, his agitation growing. "So, are you going to remove Anderson or not?"

"My price is four million," The Whistler replied coolly. "If you want Anderson removed, I can ensure that happens."

With a deliberate motion, Folly reached deep into the recesses of his heavy, tailored coat pocket, his fingers brushing against the soft fabric before gripping a thick wad of cash nestled inside. As he pulled it out, the crisp, freshly minted bills shimmered in the warm, golden light that streamed through the steam-filled room. "This is twenty thousand," he declared, his voice steady and unwavering as he placed the stack on the polished mahogany bench. "The remaining balance will be wired to your account by my assistant upon successful completion of the task."

With that, he pivoted and stepped out, the humid air swirling around him and clinging to his skin like an unwanted embrace as he exited the steam room. The soothing scent of eucalyptus lingered, evoking tranquility even amid the tension. As he navigated the tiled corridor, he unzipped his pants, urgency driving him toward the restroom. In the background, the haunting melody of The Whistler played softly, its notes weaving an almost nostalgic tapestry that whispered the unspoken secrets.

Counselor Folly returned to the table with a confident stride, his presence instantly lifting the atmosphere that had felt so heavy just moments before with the overweight man's departure. The remnants of his visit had been meticulously erased by the Counselor's efficient team, leaving the polished table surface gleaming under the soft, golden glow of the overhead lights.

Folly lifted his crystal wine glass, its facets sparkling like tiny stars as it caught the flickering reflections of the nearby candles. He held it aloft like a prized trophy, a symbol of triumph. With a mischievous grin curling at the corners of his mouth, he proclaimed, "Here's to Doyle Anderson and Deborah finally reaping what they've sown!"

"Cheers!" the group echoed in unison, their voices bursting with relief and shared excitement, the sound of clinking glasses ringing out joyfully in the cozy, intimate setting. It was a moment of celebration, electric with a sense of freedom and new beginnings.

Meanwhile, back at the Wardens' office, the atmosphere hums with an unusual energy as Deborah, Doyle, and Sonny step inside. They stride in from the gleaming landing platform, where faint echoes of their footsteps bounce off the polished walls. Doyle's eyes widen as he gazes out the large window, his expression a mix of astonishment and incredulity. "Are we really not going to discuss the fact that a dragon just spoke?" he blurts, his voice carrying the weight of disbelief.

Deborah and Sonny exchange a brief, startled look, a silent acknowledgment of the surreal moment. Still, they continue their purposeful walk toward the back office, their minds racing with the implications of what they've just witnessed.

“Hello? Did you hear me?” Doyle presses, his voice rising with urgency, the edges of his irritation sharpening as he feels his concerns brushing against the realm of absurdity.

Deborah pauses and turns to face him, her expression calm and clear amid the chaos. “Yes, we heard you,” she responds, her voice steady as she tries to ground the situation.

With a dramatic flair, Doyle throws his arms up in exasperation, the tension in his shoulders evident. “Let’s just act like it’s completely normal—first, that dragons exist, and second, that they can actually talk,” he remarks, shaking his head in disbelief, the extraordinary nature of their world swirling around him like an untamed storm.

“Up to this point, I’ve tolerated all of this absurdity,” Doyle shouted, his voice trembling with both frustration and disbelief. “AI robots are everywhere you look, whirring and whirring, and flying discs darting across the sky like errant comets. And we also have, can you believe it? ten-foot-tall Watchers, feasting on people like they’re nothing more than morsels!” His wide eyes glinted with horror as he gestured emphatically, painting a vivid picture of the chaos surrounding them.

“Darling, please, try to calm down,” Deborah urged softly, her voice a soothing balm amidst the tempest of his thoughts. She reached toward him, her hands gently coaxing him to focus.

Doyle let out a frantic, almost deranged laugh that rang out sharply against the walls. “Calm down? Have you lost your mind? Today, I’ve seen a man with four arms—four!—and another with three bulging eyes! And now we have a bizarre blue cowboy standing right in front of us, alongside a dragon that just spoke to him in a deep, rumbling voice!" His body swayed as if caught in a tempest, and he clutched his head, his fingers digging deep into his scalp in a futile attempt to steady his racing thoughts.

Deborah pushed herself forward, urgency radiating from her features like sunlight breaking through a stormy sky, but it was too late. The tidal wave of his fears crashed down upon him, an insurmountable force that pulled him under. With a muffled gasp escaping his lips, Doyle crumpled to the ground, his body hitting the floor with a heavy thud that reverberated through the air, echoing the surreal chaos of their fractured reality. As the world around him faded into shadows, Doyle's mind was swept away into a vivid flashback, dragging him into the depths of his past.

0202 HOURS
06 SEPTEMBER 2011
COMMAND CENTER, AFGHANISTAN

Doyle slipped on his headphones, the faint crackle of radio transmissions immediately filling his ears. He tuned into the voices of the Chinook's pilots and the support aircraft buzzing in the area. His heart raced as he thought to himself, "Just drop off the Delta team and get the hell out of there."

"One minute out," came the unmistakable voice of the Chinook pilot, slicing through the thick tension that enveloped the control room.

"Come on, guys. Just get on the ground!" Doyle exclaimed, his voice echoing in the cramped space, a mixture of impatience and concern. The atmosphere was electric with anxiety as he stood behind several drone operators, their eyes darting between radar blips and real-time drone footage. Meanwhile, two radar operators on the opposite side of the room monitored the unfolding situation.

"Thirty seconds out," the pilot announced, urgency in his tone.

Suddenly, a frantic shout broke the silence. "Sir, we are seeing movement near the landing zone!" an operator yelled, his eyes wide with alarm as he turned to the mission commander, who sat off to the side, a focused look etched on his face.

"What type of movement?" the commander inquired, his voice steady amidst the chaos. The mid-sized spy drones soared high above to avoid detection, while the operator strained to gain a clearer view. With steady hands, he lowered the drone's altitude and zoomed in, the camera lens adjusting to capture the unfolding scene.

Moments later, a blinding flash erupted on the screens, followed by a wave of loud static that made everyone flinch.

"What the hell was that?" Doyle shouted, his heart pounding. "It looked like an RPG fired at the Chinook!"

One of the radar operators spun around, anxiety etched on his face. "Sir, we lost contact."

With a sense of urgency, the mission commander approached the operators, his eyes narrowing. "Are the drones over that site yet?"

"Sir, there's a lot of smoke and interference," the operator replied, his brow furrowed as he struggled to regain visibility.

"Are the two support Apache helicopters in a position to report back to us?" the commander pressed, his tone firm.

"Yes, sir, they are moving closer. They want to know if they can open fire if they spot any enemy fighters," the operator responded, tension woven into his words.

"Tell them negative," the commander uttered quietly, a heavy weight in his voice.

After several tense minutes of the operator trying to pierce through the thick veil of smoke, a message crackled through from the Apache pilots. "Sir, the Apaches are over the site, and there's a large fire blazing on the ground," they reported, the reality of the situation sinking heavily in the control room.

"They've been shot down!" Doyle's voice cuts through the tension in the command center like a knife, reverberating off the stark gray walls as he slams his fists against the desk, rage and disbelief surging through him.

The commander, a seasoned veteran with a weathered face marked by years of conflict, leans closer to the array of flickering screens displaying live feeds from the chaotic battlefield. His eyes narrow as he scans for any sign of hope amid the turmoil. "Turn that volume up," he instructs sharply, urgency infusing his voice.

From the crackling radio, the voice of Apache Pilot B breaks through the static, filled with anxiety. "Do you see any survivors?" he asks, the weight of his question hanging in the air.

Apache Pilot A responds, his tone edged with fear, "Negative, I'm not seeing any. Shit, it's engulfed in flames!" The vivid scene he describes flashes in the minds of those in the room—a fiery inferno consuming twisted metal, with smoke rising into the sky like sorrowful billows.

Pilot A continues, his voice tense with adrenaline, "I see four Taliban fighters fleeing the scene. Permission to engage?"

"Negative, do not engage," the operator intercepts, his voice steady but firm. The gravity of the situation presses down on him. The command center buzzes with frenzied activity as analysts track movements on the screens and operators relay critical updates to the pilots and the elite 75th Ranger Regiment on the ground, their faces a mix of determination and worry.

Doyle, fully aware of the gravity of the moment, feels a surge of responsibility. He must mobilize the Trail-Finder team, a specialized unit renowned for its courage in recovering downed aircraft in hostile environments. With a sense of urgency, he removes his headset; the sudden silence amplifies the tension around him. He strides purposefully out of the command center and into the dim, claustrophobic office nearby. There, the walls are lined with maps and mission briefings that echo the weight of every previous operation.

He picks up the phone, his voice intense and clipped as he arranges the details with the team leader. After a brief conversation filled with concise responses and urgent arrangements, he hangs up, determination hardening his features, and strides back into the command center.

The commander approaches him, concern etched deeply into every line of his face. "We just received word that the 75th is moving to the crash site," he informs Doyle, urgency matching the racing thoughts in the room.

"I told you we were using the wrong equipment," Doyle snaps back, frustration bubbling beneath the surface as the reality of their situation looms large, casting a shadow over their plans and the lives at stake.

The commander jabbed his finger at Doyle, his expression tight with frustration. "I'm not going to debate this with you right now. Just do your damn job!"

Doyle stood tall, defiance etched on his face. "I always do my damn job, Sir! So why didn't we engage the fighters who fired at the helicopter?" he demanded, his voice rising with emotion. The tension in the air crackled as their eyes locked, both men unwilling to back down.

1930 HOURS
PRESENT-DAY
THE WARDENS OFFICE, THE SEWER DISTRICT

"Doyle, I know you always do your job," Deborah said softly, her voice a gentle balm amidst the chaos.

Doyle blinked as he slowly opened his eyes, taking in the sight of Deborah and Sonny kneeling beside him. The dim light cast a warm glow on their concerned faces, and Deborah's hand gently enveloped his.

With careful support, they helped him sit up, and Deborah, her expression filled with compassion, offered him a cup of water. "I've infused this water with some special ingredients to help calm your racing thoughts," she explained, her tone both reassuring and earnest. "We have medications in The Sewer District that are restricted in your world, but they really do work."

The warm liquid in the cup felt like a lifeline in that moment, promising relief from the storm inside his mind.

"You need to forgive yourself for what happened to your friends," Deborah said, her voice calm and reassuring as Doyle took a slow sip from his cup. Lights streamed through the window, filling the room with a warm, golden glow that contrasted sharply with the heaviness of their discussion. "Jonah has done an excellent job of helping you realize that the world around you is not what you were taught to believe in school."

Doyle set the cup down on his lap, his hands trembling slightly as he grappled with his thoughts. "I understand. I truly regret losing my temper."

Deborah let out a gentle laugh, her eyes sparkling with warmth. "That's perfectly understandable, darling. In times of emotional turmoil, it's easy to feel overwhelmed. I promise to share more with you as we continue on this journey, but for now, we need to focus. It's time to head out and meet The Driver and Eddie at the church."

Doyle rises from the floor, adjusting his jacket to ensure it sits neatly on his shoulders as he spots a small drone gliding toward him. The drone hovers gently in the air, cradling his hat—an elegant fedora—that had fallen from his head during the exhilarating ride on the flying bike. With a swift motion, he reaches out, grasping the hat from the drone's delicate grasp. A smile crosses his face as he looks at the mechanical helper and says, “Thank you,” appreciating the unexpected assistance.

“Follow us, Doyle,” Deborah urged, her voice echoing softly as she stepped out of the Warden’s office, making her way down the dimly lit corridor. “We’re catching the train to the church.”

“Train?” Doyle asked, raising an eyebrow in confusion.

“Yes,” Deborah replied, a hint of excitement in her tone. “It’s a charming little train that glides through a sleek, underground tube, connecting the Wardens’ block to the entrance of The Sewer District. We host esteemed dignitaries from Atlantis here almost daily, showcasing our unique and vibrant culture.”

As she spoke, the faint rumble of the train rose in the distance, promising an intriguing journey ahead.

CHAPTER FIVE

THE PIRATE SHIP

2000 HOURS
PRESENT-DAY
THE SHIPYARD, ATLANTIS

Deborah and Doyle gathered with the crew at the ornate church, its stone façade illuminated by the warm glow of lantern light as twilight enveloped the city in a velvety embrace. They stepped into a sleek elevator that hummed softly as it ascended to the vibrant streets of Atlantis.

Upon reaching street level, they noticed a futuristic flying taxi awaiting them, its aerodynamic design and smooth surface shimmering under the softening glow of neon lights. As night fell gracefully, the city came alive with a kaleidoscope of colors, each window and streetlamp twinkling like stars against the darkening sky.

Above them, the aerial roadways were bustling with traffic, an intricate dance of vehicles gliding effortlessly through the air, their lights streaking past like shooting stars. The AI taxi driver, a sophisticated piece of technology, navigated the busy skies with precision, weaving through countless flying cars on its way to the lively Shipyard District of Atlantis. The rhythmic sounds of machinery and the briny scent of the sea mingled in the night air, promising adventure and excitement ahead.

Deborah turned to Doyle, the hum of the three-row flying taxi enveloping them in a cocoon of modernity and comfort. Plush seats cradled their bodies as they soared above the dazzling city, its lights shimmering like a cascade of diamonds. She studied Doyle's expression, noting the flicker of uncertainty in his eyes. "You have to unlearn everything you've learned to accept throughout your life," she said, her voice resonating with earnest conviction. "Much of what you've absorbed from the nightly news is nothing but a carefully crafted facade, designed to manipulate your perception of reality." The air crackled with the weight of her words as the taxi glided smoothly through the night sky.

The medication that Deborah had administered to Doyle was beginning to take effect, gently lifting the veil of confusion from his mind. He looked at her, his eyes reflecting a newfound clarity. "I realize now that the world I thought I knew is actually vast and intricate, far more complex than I ever understood," he confessed, his voice tinged with awe.

Deborah smiled softly, her expression warm and reassuring. "The world you used to inhabit kept God hidden from your sight. But in this expansive reality, his presence cannot be easily overlooked," she explained, her voice carrying the weight of profound truth.

The air taxi slowed and dropped away from the frenetic pace of the traffic high in the sky and entered a serene stretch by the waterfront. "Doyle, just look at those magnificent ships; those are the formidable vessels that Atlantis utilizes for its bustling commerce and trade," Deborah said, her voice brimming with excitement.

Doyle turned to gaze out the window, his breath hitching at the breathtaking sight before him. Enormous sailing ships floated regally in the harbor, their towering masts soaring into the sky like ancient trees reaching for the heavens. Each ship featured three grand masts, adorned with vast sails that billowed gracefully in the brisk maritime breeze, reflecting the setting sunlight in a dazzling array of whites and golds. "I can hardly believe my eyes! They're even larger than aircraft carriers!" Doyle exclaimed, his voice filled with wonder as he absorbed the awe-inspiring spectacle of maritime engineering.

Deborah gestured toward the massive ships, "They have to be that large because of the sheer size of the creatures living here," she explained, her voice steady and knowledgeable, revealing her familiarity with the ocean's secrets.

Doyle, mesmerized by the sight of the sleek vessels gliding effortlessly across the waves, leaned in with wide eyes filled with wonder. "Why do they use sails? Why don't these ships operate solely on nuclear power?"

"These ships are powered by nuclear energy," Deborah replied, her eyes sparkling with intrigue. "However, when they venture into areas known to be plagued by Krakens, the crew opts for sails as a strategic precaution. It's a critical safety measure."

"Krakens? I thought they were having a laugh at my expense," Doyle responded, disbelief coloring his tone.

Deborah shook her head softly, her expression shifting to one of earnest seriousness. "No, darling, they weren't laughing. Krakens are real, and they're attracted to vibrations and sounds. Once they target a ship, the best way to evade them is to go completely silent and rely on the sails. These sails, interestingly enough, are constructed from a light metal alloy that not only captures the wind but also serves as a radar system, allowing the ship to communicate its position and navigate effectively."

The taxi arrived at the dock, where a massive black ship loomed majestically against the backdrop of the shimmering water. "We built this ship as a replica of Queen Anne's Revenge, but ten times larger," Deborah explained, her voice filled with pride as she gestured toward the vessel's intricate details.

"Blackbeard's ship," Doyle responded, his eyes widening in awe at the sheer scale and dark beauty of the craft.

"That's correct," Deborah replied, a gleam of excitement in her eyes, as the taxi came to a halt and the doors swung open, ready to welcome them aboard this grand tribute to history.

Doyle stepped out of the taxi and was greeted by an AI deckhand, who promptly handed him his bag. "Thank you," he said, nodding in appreciation to the efficient deckhand. Turning to Deborah, he curiously asked, "What type of material is the ship made from?"

With a warm smile, Deborah replied, "It's not constructed from traditional steel. Instead, the ship is built from a state-of-the-art composite material. This innovative substance offers remarkable strength that surpasses that of steel while weighing less than half as much, allowing for greater speed and maneuverability on the water."

Doyle carefully followed The Driver and Sonny up the gleaming metal ramp leading to the ship's entrance. Behind them, Eddie the drone hovered gently, while Deborah moved with purpose, her expression reflecting a mix of anticipation and determination.

As they stepped onto the polished deck, the captain warmly greeted them, a distinguished figure with a weathered face and an inviting smile. "Welcome aboard once again, Deborah," he said, tipping his hat in a gesture of respect.

"Thank you, Captain," she replied, returning the smile with genuine warmth.

The captain snapped his fingers sharply, and in an instant, four AI crew members, sleek and efficient in their design, presented themselves before the group. "My crew will take your men to their cabins," he announced, gesturing with a nod of his head.

"Thank you, Captain," Deborah responded, her voice steady and appreciative.

Addressing Deborah directly, the captain continued, "You, my lady, will enjoy the comfort of an executive suite situated on the captain's deck." His tone conveyed both hospitality and a hint of pride in the accommodations.

"The drone, however, I'm uncertain where he will stay," the captain remarked, a trace of concern lacing his voice, his brow furrowing slightly as he surveyed the bustling deck.

"I have a perfect spot for him; he can stay with me in my cabin," Doyle replied with a confident smile, casting a casual glance at the drone that hovered eagerly near his shoulder, its sensors whirring softly.

The captain let out a hearty chuckle, the tension dissipating like morning fog in the sun. "Very well then. It is settled."

"This way, gentlemen," a crew member announced with a respectful nod, gesturing toward the walkway. Doyle, The Driver, and Sonny closely followed him across the expansive deck, where the salty breeze danced around them, bringing with it the invigorating scent of the open sea. The warm deck lights illuminated their path, casting a soft glow over the ship's metal surfaces, while Eddie, the drone, hummed softly, as if attuned to the moment's excitement.

Together, they descended the staircase, the crew member leading them into a dimly lit corridor. Doors lined the hallway every ten feet, each one concealing a small sanctuary for weary sailors seeking respite from their toils. The atmosphere was rich with the faint, briny scent of ocean air, intertwined with the comforting aroma of polished metal and the faintest hint of engine oil, a testament to the ship's rigorous daily operations and the stories held within its sturdy hull.

Deborah stood at the edge of the deck, her eyes catching the sleek silhouette of a black limousine as it glided to a stop. The air was thick with the scent of saltwater and the distant hum of the city. Two deckhands approached the vehicle and engaged in a brief conversation with a sharply dressed man who sat in the back seat. As the trunk of the limo popped open with a soft thud, one of the deckhands stepped forward, retrieving a long, elegantly wrapped box.

He carefully maneuvered it onto the ramp, its polished surface glinting under the dock's ambient lights. Clutching the package, he ascended the ramp with purpose before presenting it to one of the ship's crew members, who accepted it with a nod of gratitude.

The crew member then made his way toward Deborah, his footsteps echoing against the metal planks. "Jonah wanted you to have this, my lady," he said, handing over the box with a respectful bow.

"Thank you," Deborah replied, her curiosity piqued as she turned to glance back at the limousine. Through the tinted window, she caught a glimpse of Jonah, who raised his hand in a friendly wave. As the window rolled shut with a gentle hum, the limousine accelerated away, climbing gracefully into the starry sky and vanishing into the bustling traffic of lights that populated the evening.

"The beautiful women always receive gifts," the captain remarked with a charming smile as he looked at Deborah. "Now, if you will follow me, I'll guide you to your luxurious suite, and then we can set sail on our grand adventure," he explained, his voice warm and inviting.

"Thank you, Captain," she replied, her eyes sparkling with excitement.

With an air of authority, the captain, flanked by two attentive crew members in crisp uniforms, led Deborah up to the captain's deck. The city lights shimmered on the water, giving everything a golden hue as they approached one of the elegant executive suites. The crew members stood proudly on either side of the door, their expressions respectful as the captain swung it open to reveal the sumptuous interior.

"My lady, if you would be so gracious as to join me in my private dining room for dinner in one hour," the captain said, bowing slightly as he took her hand, bringing it to his lips for a soft kiss. His gaze lingered on her, filled with a blend of admiration and intrigue.

"Thank you, Captain. How will I find my way to the dining room?" Deborah inquired, her brows slightly furrowed in curiosity.

"I will dispatch these two crew members to guide you in about forty-five minutes," the Captain explained.

"I'm looking forward to it," she replied, her face lighting up with a warm smile as she pictured the excitement of the unfolding adventure.

Deborah closed the heavy metal door to her luxurious suite, the soft click echoing in the quiet atmosphere as she untied her clothing. She stepped into the refreshing cascade of the shower, the warm water enveloping her and washing away the tension of anticipation for her dinner date. As the water streamed down her shoulders, she felt the subtle movement of the ship beneath her, gently being towed away from the dock and into the deeper waters beyond the shallows.

Meanwhile, in a modest cabin not far from hers, Doyle sat comfortably on a small sofa, his gaze fixed on Eddie, the drone, which rested on a table beside him. They engaged in a focused conversation with The Driver, who leaned against the wall, arms crossed.

"It will take us all night to reach the island where the flying disk crashed," The Driver explained, his tone serious as he glanced at a map spread out on the table.

Doyle raised an eyebrow, curiosity piqued. "Are we going to dine with the crew tonight?" he asked, hoping for a chance to mingle with the ship's staff.

The Driver nodded, his expression softening. "Yes, one of the crew members will meet us in the hall in half an hour. I'll return to my cabin to prepare, and I'll see you then."

After her shower, Deborah emerged, feeling revitalized. She draped herself in a stunning ballroom gown, the fabric shimmering softly under the cabin lights. As she paced back and forth in her suite, the anticipation gnawed at her. Something about the evening felt off. "Something doesn't feel right," she whispered to herself, a sense of unease settling in her gut as shadows flickered in the dim light.

A loud, unexpected knock at the door made Deborah jump, her heart racing for a moment. She walked to the entrance and opened it to find two crew members standing there, their uniforms crisp and polished.

"My lady, if you would follow us, please," one of them said, his tone respectful and inviting.

"Of course," Deborah replied, a curious excitement bubbling within her as she stepped into the softly lit corridor. The scent of salt-water lingered in the air, mingling with the rich aroma of a delicious meal wafting from just ahead.

They led her a short distance to the captain's private dining room, where the captain stood waiting. He was tall and commanding, and as he approached her, admiration lit his face.

"You look absolutely stunning tonight," he said, his voice warm and genuine, as he took in the elegant dress that flowed gracefully around her.

"Thank you," she replied, a flutter of warmth rising to her cheeks as the crew members quietly left, pulling the door shut behind them. She heard the faint click of a lock, a sound that momentarily stirred an uneasy feeling within her.

The captain stepped closer, a confident smile playing on his lips as he reached out to put his arms around her.

"You also smell delightful," he remarked, his gaze lingering on her as if drinking in her presence.

Deborah instinctively pushed him away, attempting to regain her composure. "What are we having for dinner tonight?" she asked, shifting the focus away from the tension in the air.

The captain gestured toward the dining table, which glistened under the warm glow of the chandelier, laden with a lavish spread of culinary delights. "We have crab and cod expertly prepared, along with mouthwatering salmon and succulent shrimp. Everything your heart could desire," he said, his eyes sparkling with enthusiasm as he moved closer to her once again, the enticing scent of the feast drawing her in.

"Shall we eat?" she asked, her voice inviting.

"I prefer to start with dessert," the captain replied, his tone sultry and low as he deftly unzipped his pants with a confident flick of his wrist. He stepped closer to Deborah, his presence commanding as he guided her firmly and bent her over the large, polished table. The soft fabric of her dress cascaded down her shoulders, pooling at her waist like a silken waterfall, while his hands pushed aside her undergarments, as tension filled the air.

"Please stop!" she shouted, her voice a mix of surprise and defiance.

"Hold still," the captain commanded, kicking her legs apart with an assertive gesture.

In a flash, Deborah tapped into her remarkable strength. With surprising agility, she wrapped her legs around the captain's, turning her body to confront him. She reached up, her fingers curling around his throat, and stood tall, her posture fierce. The hem of her dress slipped down to her ankles, leaving her clad only in her panties, her bare skin glistening under the dim light. With her large breasts exposed and eyes fierce, she locked her gaze with the captain's, an unspoken challenge igniting the air between them.

"Who do you work for?" she inquired, her voice steady as she seized his genitals with one hand, applying pressure that made him wince.

The captain gasped, "The Whistler hired me for Counselor Folly."

A cold smile spread across Deborah's face. "That's what I suspected. Take a good look at these breasts; they are the last you will ever see," she said, her grip tightening around his throat. With a swift, calculated motion, she snapped his neck, ending his life in an instant.

Deborah carefully maneuvers his body into one of the sturdy diner chairs, gently placing his head on the table, resting it on his arms as if he has indulged a bit too much in the evening's festivities.

She glances around the room, her heart racing, before retrieving her elegant dress from the floor, sliding into it with practiced ease. As she catches her reflection in one of the shiny diner plates, she skillfully touches up her makeup, making sure to restore her polished appearance.

With a flicker of determination, she pulls a sleek phone from her purse and types a quick message, her fingers moving rapidly across the screen.

Meanwhile, in the larger dining room, The Driver sits at a table with Doyle and Sonny, engaged in light conversation, when he suddenly feels a subtle vibration coming from his phone. He discreetly extracts it from his pocket and reads the message, a furrow of concentration forming on his brow. Looking briefly at Doyle, he says, "If you would excuse me," before standing up. He strides confidently out of the dining room, making his way to the captain's deck, where the cool evening air awaits.

The Driver stepped onto the captain's deck with a careful, measured gait, his senses heightened as he surveyed his surroundings for any signs of movement. The soft hum of the ship's machinery filled the air as he spotted two crew members lingering near the ornate door of the captain's dining room, their casual chatter echoing slightly in the enclosed space.

With a flicker of determination in his eyes, he retrieved a small device from his pocket, the cool metal glinting under the dim overhead lights. He tossed it lightly into the air, watching as it soared with a quiet whir. The drone, a compact marvel of technology, navigated expertly to the other entrance of the captain's deck. It paused momentarily, capturing the scene before it, and then erupted in a stunning burst of bright flashes, a dazzling distraction against the muted backdrop of the ship's interior.

Startled by the explosion of light, the two crew members quickly abandoned their post, rushing towards the source of the ruckus, their hurried footsteps echoing across the polished floor. Seizing the moment, The Driver darted towards the captain's dining room door. His heart raced as he swiftly unlocked it, the latch clicking softly in the lock before he slipped inside, leaving the chaos behind.

"What's wrong?" The Driver inquired, his brow furrowing with concern.

Deborah, trembling slightly, pointed toward the captain slumped motionless at the table, a grim expression on her face. "He tried to rape me."

The Driver's face flushed with anger, turning a deep crimson as his eyes narrowed. "That no-good..." he muttered, clenching his fists and taking a determined step toward the captain who lay lifeless.

Deborah swiftly reached out, her grip firm as she held him back. "Stop. He's dead. I broke his neck."

The Driver paused, disbelief etched across his features as he scanned her face for any signs of distress. "Are you okay?"

"Of course I am," she replied, her voice steady and resolute. "The captain wasn't strong enough to do anything to me."

"Who is he?" The Driver inquired, his brow furrowing with concern.

Deborah retrieved a cigarette from her purse, the flick of her lighter casting a brief glow as she ignited it. "I'm not entirely sure," she replied, exhaling a plume of smoke into the dimly lit room. "He claimed to work for The Whistler and Folly, but I don't know what he did with the real captain. For now, it appears that you're the captain."

The Driver stood still for a moment, absorbing the weight of the situation. "I can manage that," he said with a steady resolve. "We'll need to reprogram the AI crew to recognize me as the captain. Their compliance will be crucial moving forward."

Deborah took a long draw from her cigarette, contemplating the implications. "I'll get right on it. But we must remain vigilant; there could be more of Folly's men lurking about the ship. You mustn't breathe a word of this to Doyle or Sonny. Do you understand?" she asked, her tone serious and commanding.

"Yes, ma'am. I understand completely," he responded, determination etched across his face.

"I will inform Doyle when the moment is appropriate," Deborah stated with a determined tone as she stepped closer to the lifeless form of the captain. "We need to remove his uniform so you can disguise yourself in it."

The Driver nodded, his expression serious, and together they carefully stripped the captain of his clothing. Once they removed the uniform, the Driver quickly donned it, adjusting the cuffs and smoothing out any wrinkles to make it presentable.

Deborah surveyed the area and then turned toward the adjoining kitchen. Her eyes scanned the small, cluttered space until they landed on a narrow closet tucked away in the corner. With a sense of urgency, she moved to the closet, opened the door, and cleared out some kitchen supplies before gently placing the captain's body inside, ensuring he was well-hidden. With a final glance around the room, she knew they had to act fast to reprogram the AI crew before anyone discovered their secret.

"I will need Eddie the drone to reprogram the crew. Can you please have him come to my suite?" she requested, her tone firm yet composed as she addressed The Driver.

"At once, ma'am," The Driver replied, promptly reaching for his phone with practiced efficiency.

Meanwhile, Eddie, the small, intelligent drone, rested on a polished wooden table in Doyle's cabin, his metallic surface gleaming in the soft cabin light. As he completed his charging cycle, his lights blinked to life, and with a gentle whir, he took off, gliding smoothly out of the room.

Deborah approached the captain's dining room door and rapped her knuckles against its solid surface, awaiting a response from the crew. Moments later, two crew members grabbed the doorknob, their expressions a mix of confusion and surprise. "Did you unlock this door?" one inquired, glancing at the other.

"No," the second crew member replied, shaking his head as they opened the door to allow her passage.

"Thank you," Deborah said graciously, nodding her head in acknowledgment as she stepped past them and made her way back to her suite, her heels clicking softly against the floor.

Meanwhile, The Driver remained seated at the table, his back to the crew, exuding authority.

"Is there anything else, sir?" one of the crew members ventured to inquire, breaking the silence that hung in the air.

Without turning around, The Driver waved his hand dismissively, signaling for them to exit the room and resume their duties.

Deborah stood anxiously by her door, her heart racing as she awaited Eddie's arrival. When she finally spotted him approaching, she flung the door open to welcome him inside and swiftly closed it behind him, ensuring their conversation remained private.

"Eddie," she began, her voice steady yet urgent, "I need you to access the main computer and reprogram the crew's settings to recognize The Driver as the new captain. Here is the security code for his badge." She handed him a small card bearing the code, her expression serious.

"Yes, ma'am," Eddie responded, as he scanned the card, fully aware of the gravity of her request.

Deborah fixed her gaze on him, her eyes intense with conviction. "It's crucial that you do not disclose this information to anyone, especially not to Doyle, until I've had the opportunity to explain the transition to him personally." She paused, aware of the risks involved. "This is a sensitive operation, and we need to handle it carefully."

Deborah stepped forward and carefully opened the ornate box that Jonah had delivered earlier, its intricate carvings catching the dim light in the suite. With a sense of purpose, she reached inside and retrieved her magical staff, its polished surface gleaming as she held it aloft. She turned to Eddie, who had already hooked into the main computer, the soft glow of the screen illuminating his polished surface. "I'll be right back," she said, her voice steady and firm.

With that, Deborah walked into the hallway, her high-heeled shoes echoing softly against the polished floor as she approached the two crew members stationed by the dining room door. They stood rigidly, tension evident in the way they shifted their weight. "Excuse me," she began, her tone carrying an edge of authority. "You two locked the door as soon as I entered. What prompted that decision?"

"Ma'am?" one of the crew members replied, confusion flickering across his face, just as Deborah swung her staff with precise, lethal intent, the magic within it crackling to life as it cleanly severed both of their heads from their bodies. The sudden violence hung in the air, and The Driver, startled by the commotion, emerged from the dining room, his instincts honed as he processed the shocking scene.

Deborah turned to him, her expression unwavering. "Dispose of their bodies in the closet with the captain," she instructed, her voice calm and commanding. "Once we're further out to sea, we can cast them into the ocean, ensuring they vanish without a trace." The Driver nodded, a mix of shock and resolve on his face, as he prepared to carry out her orders. "This is going to be my kind of trip. We're barely away from the dock, and three bodies have already hit the floor," he replied, smiling.

CHAPTER SIX

VOYAGE ON THE SEAS

2300 HOURS
PRESENT-DAY
THE GULF OF ATLANTIS

Doyle reclines in a weathered chair on the expansive deck of the grand replica of the Queen Anne's Revenge. He puffs on a final cigar, the rich, earthy smoke swirling around him like a ghostly companion. The crisp evening breeze carries a hint of salt from the sea, intertwining with the robust scent of tobacco, creating an atmosphere that is both calming and reflective.

They have been at sea for two hours, and the twinkling lights of Atlantis have long since slipped below the horizon, swallowed by the vast expanse of the darkening sky. The ocean stretches out like a polished mirror, perfectly reflecting the star-studded canopy above, while a gentle breeze caresses the surface, creating delicate ripples. The ship, a marvel of engineering powered by cutting-edge nuclear energy, glides silently through the water, its sails neatly furled and hugging the masts with precision, ready for the next burst of wind.

The tranquility of the night envelops them, creating a profound sense of isolation and adventure amidst the endless sea.

Doyle is worried about The Driver's abrupt departure, leaving a tense silence that still hangs in the air. Deborah's lively laughter, usually the highlight of their gatherings, is also missing, creating an unsettling void. Not even Eddie, the drone, has been seen.

In a nearby chair, Sonny, the enigmatic blue-skinned tracker, sits wrapped in his thoughts, his presence commanding yet silently reserved. He is absorbed in the gentle ritual of smoking a long, slender pipe, the tendrils of aromatic smoke drifting lazily into the night sky, merging with the stars like whispers of secrets shared. Though he hasn't spoken, his sharp, observant eyes seem to take in every detail, every movement, as though he is attuned to an unseen energy surrounding them.

Above, the stars shimmer with an astonishing brilliance, their intricate patterns and elusive forms almost beckoning Doyle to decipher their celestial secrets. Each constellation seems to pulse with life, casting a soft, ethereal glow that contrasts with the deepening shadows of the night. A sense of mystery hangs heavy in the air, drawing Doyle into a world of contemplation where the stories of the past come to life amid a tranquil yet charged atmosphere.

"Beautiful night, isn't it?" Doyle asks Sonny, his voice laced with curiosity as he gauges whether Sonny will engage. Sonny takes a deep puff from his pipe, the fragrant smoke curling lazily into the cool evening air, his gaze fixed on the horizon. "Something is coming," he murmurs, a hint of unease threading through his words.

Doyle gazed out across the sea. "I don't see anything, Sonny," he remarked, turning back to his companion. Sonny continued to stare straight ahead, not responding. Doyle shifted his gaze back to the ocean and took a puff from his cigar. "Strange guy," he thought to himself.

"There you are," Deborah called cheerfully as she stepped onto the starlit deck, the salty sea breeze tousling her hair. The sudden sound of her voice startled Doyle, causing him to jump slightly in surprise.

"You scared me!" he exclaimed, a broad grin spreading across his face as he tried to catch his breath.

Sonny, now leaning against the railing and gazing thoughtfully at the endless expanse of the ocean, turned to glance at Deborah before returning his attention to the shimmering waves. "I hope you two have been enjoying some engaging conversations this beautiful evening," she said, her tone warm and inviting.

Doyle chuckled, his eyes twinkling with mischief. "Oh, you know it! Sonny won't stop talking," he replied, playfully rolling his eyes.

Deborah smiled, "What he doesn't say speaks volumes."

"Where have you been? And have you seen The Driver or Eddie?" Doyle inquired, concern creasing his brow.

Deborah slid a chair next to Doyle and settled into it with a weary sigh. "We've been overwhelmed," she explained, glancing around the room as if to ensure they were alone. "Folly had one of his enforcers impersonating the captain of this ship. The Driver, Eddie, and I took matters into our own hands and dealt with him."

Doyle raised an eyebrow, intrigued. "What do you mean by 'dealt with him'?"

Deborah reached into her purse and pulled out a cigarette, the movement deliberate. "Let's just say, he's now taking a permanent break from commanding the crew. He feeds the fish now," she said with a smirk, lighting the cigarette and inhaling deeply.

At that moment, Sonny returned to his chair, a knowing grin on his face. He chuckled softly, shaking his head. "I told you something was coming, didn't I?"

"Where are the other two?" Doyle inquired, a note of concern threading through his voice as he glanced around the dimly lit deck, shadows dancing on the walls.

"The Driver has assumed command of this ship, navigating us through the vastness of this sea with confidence, while Eddie has retreated to your cabin to recharge and recalibrate. He needed to reprogram the AI crew to acknowledge The Driver as their new captain," Deborah elaborated, her tone calm and informative, her gaze fixed on the stars twinkling like diamonds outside the massive viewport.

Doyle nodded, his shoulders easing as the weight of uncertainty lifted. "I see. That certainly eases my mind. With that settled, I think I'll turn in and try to catch some sleep before morning dawns."

Deborah tilted her head slightly, her eyes sparkling with mischief. "I have ample room in my suite, and my bed is particularly inviting, should you choose to join me."

Doyle sat up straighter in his chair, incredulity etched across his features. "Why must you persistently harass me in such a sexually provocative manner?"

With a deliberate, slow draw from her cigarette, Deborah exhaled a plume of smoke that swirled around her like a silvery veil. "Darling, I am half hybrid, part fallen angel, to be precise. We possess a profound and often uncontrollable desire for earthly men. I do my utmost to keep it in check, but it's a longing that will never truly subside."

Doyle rose from his seat, a playful glint in his eye, and remarked, "Well, do your best to improve at not doing that," as he strolled past her. Just as he reached the level of her chair, Deborah playfully reached out and delivered a light smack to his rear end. Doyle halted, letting out an exaggerated sigh, "That's not exactly helping you get better!"

Deborah couldn't help but let out a soft, melodic laugh as Doyle walked away, the sound of her amusement mixing with Sonny's chuckles in the background, creating a warm and lively atmosphere.

Doyle walked back to his cozy cabin, the soft lights casting warm shadows across the room. As he entered, he spotted Eddie, his trusted drone, perched on the nightstand, quietly recharging after a day of work. A smile tugged at the corners of Doyle's mouth, fond memories of their recent adventures flooding his mind.

After a long day, he slowly undressed, the fabric of his clothes sliding away as he prepared for rest. He climbed into the inviting warmth of his bed, the familiar comfort wrapping around him like a soft blanket. Within minutes, the gentle rhythm of his breathing signaled that he had succumbed to the peaceful embrace of slumber, leaving the drone to its silent watch over the night.

As the profound shadows of night enveloped the boundless ocean, the massive ship glided through the water, its hull cutting through the waves with an almost eerie tranquility. It sailed toward the legendary island, shrouded in mystery and marked by the remnants of the flying disk that had crash-landed there.

On the bridge, The Driver paced with a heightened sense of urgency, the rhythmic sound of his boots echoing off the polished metal floor. The soft hum of the ship's engines, intertwined with the gentle lapping of waves against the hull, created a backdrop of serenity, challenged only by the tempest of his thoughts. He observed the AI pilots at their posts, their screens flickering with data as they navigated through the inky darkness. Their movements were fluid and precise, a ballet of technology executing the delicate task of guiding the vessel safely through these treacherous waters.

Every few moments, The Driver's gaze shifted to the radar screen, a swirl of green blips and eerie echoes, tension coiling in his gut as he scanned for any sign of Krakens, ancient sea monsters known to strike fear into the hearts of sailors. He remained on high alert, understanding that beneath the calm surface, untold dangers could lurk, ready to surge forth from the depths of legend and plunge the ship into chaos.

Hours later the sudden deceleration of the ship jolted Doyle awake, pulling him from the depths of sleep. He rolled over, the coolness of the metal bed frame sending a shiver up his spine, and glanced at the small, dimly lit clock on the nightstand. "0300," he murmured to himself, the eerie quiet of the ship amplifying the reality of the late hour.

As he sat up, the absence of the soft hum of machinery signaled to Eddie, Doyle's ever-watchful drone, that it was time to come to life. Its lights blinked rhythmically, casting a flickering glow across the cabin walls.

"Doyle, my systems indicate that there is an alert," Eddie informed him, the mechanical voice cutting through the stillness with an urgent clarity.

Instantly, adrenaline surged through Doyle's veins. He leaped out of bed, his bare feet meeting the cold, metallic floor with a sense of urgency. He quickly pulled on his pants and slipped his arms into his button-up shirt, each movement deliberate and swift. Without pausing to put on his socks or boots, he charged out of the cabin, feeling an instinctive need to confront whatever awaited him in the silent corridors of the ship.

Doyle stepped out onto the ship's deck, greeted by a thick, enveloping fog that obscured his surroundings with a ghostly embrace. The small lanterns lining the deck flickered softly, casting an ambient glow that illuminated Deborah and Sonny, who remained comfortably seated in their chairs, seemingly undisturbed by the passing hours since Doyle had last seen them.

"Do you two never sleep?" Doyle asked, his voice echoing slightly in the stillness of the night as he took in the surreal scene.

"Sleep isn't necessary for hybrids," Deborah replied, her voice smooth and melodic, a hint of amusement threading through her words as if she were sharing a secret about a world unknown to him.

Doubt and curiosity mingled in Doyle's mind, prompting him to ask, "What's going on?"

Deborah's slender finger pointed toward the rear of the ship, where powerful spotlights sliced through the fog, illuminating a massive, ominous vessel that loomed before them like a phantom from a bygone era. Its hull was battered and worn, with streaks of rust running like tears down its sides. Decaying ropes hung limp from the frayed rigging, and the once-proud sails were now tattered remnants, fluttering weakly in the damp breeze.

"It's a ghost ship," Deborah said, her tone taking on a haunting quality, "and the fog is trailing behind it like a specter, as if it is guiding the lost back to their final resting place."

Doyle felt a shiver run down his spine as he gazed at the forlorn vessel, its presence evoking a deep sense of mystery and foreboding, leaving him to wonder what untold tales and secrets lay hidden within its shadows and depths.

"What do we need to do?" Doyle asked, his voice barely above a whisper as he peered into the thick, swirling fog that enveloped their ship.

"There's nothing we can do but remain silent," Deborah replied, her gaze fixed on the ominous shadows that danced in the mist. "Legend has it that Krakens often follow ghost ships, using the fog as their shroud. The Driver and the crew are currently scanning the area, searching for the great beast lurking beneath the waves."

As they spoke, the ghost ship drifted past Doyle, its tattered sails billowing like ethereal wings mere feet from their own vessel. Doyle's heart raced as he took in its immense size. "That boat is massive," he said in awe, the eerie sight leaving him spellbound.

The ghost ship silently veered away from their vessel, gliding effortlessly eastward, its eerie presence seemingly absorbing the thick fog that had enveloped them. As the night sky gradually cleared, revealing a tapestry of twinkling stars, the spectral vessel melded into the darkness, leaving no trace behind. In that moment, Doyle felt the nuclear engine's hum return with a renewed vigor, a reassuring reminder of its power. Just like that, the unsettling event faded into memory, and the boat resumed its steady course through the calm waters.

Doyle turned to face Deborah, but before he could say a word, a massive wave surged over the railing, crashing down with the force of a freight train and knocking him onto the slick deck. Instinctively, he gripped the railing with white-knuckled determination, fighting to avoid the wave from pulling him into the abyss below. As he rolled onto his back, his eyes widened in disbelief at the sight before him: an extraordinary creature unlike anything he had ever seen. The immense, undulating form of the mythical beast loomed dramatically in the churning water, its tentacles thrashing against the turbulent sea. Just then, Sonny's voice pierced through the chaos, ringing with a mix of awe and terror. "It's a Kraken!"

Lying on his back, Doyle squinted against the water in his eyes. He surveyed the deck, his pulse quickening as he became aware of two massive tentacles looming ominously from the ocean's depths. They writhed and twisted, their slick, dark skin glistening with moisture as they climbed the ship's main mast, coiling tightly around the steel structure. The sound of metal creaking under pressure sent a shiver down his spine. "It's going to drag the ship straight down into the abyss!" he heard Deborah shout, her voice rife with terror as she desperately urged Sonny to act. The atmosphere was charged with fear as the threat of disaster loomed ever closer.

Doyle sprang to his feet, his eyes trailing after Deborah as she hurriedly made her way back toward her suite. "Where are you going?" he shouted, his voice barely cutting through the din of chaos around them. The ship lurched dangerously to port, sending him reeling once more as he struggled to maintain his balance. Just then, his feet struck the slick rail, perilously close to one of the colossal tentacles of the massive Kraken that loomed beneath the surface, its presence sending a shiver down his spine.

Doyle reached into his pocket, fingers brushing against the cool metal of his small pocket knife. The blade glinted in the chaotic light as he unsheathed it, determination flooding his veins. He lunged forward, aiming for the thick, sinuous tentacle that writhed ominously beside him, its surface slick and glistening. Just as he made contact, a dark shadow loomed overhead; the Kraken swung another tentacle with terrifying speed and strength, striking Doyle with a bone-jarring force. He crashed against the metal deck, the impact knocking the breath from his body and leaving him gasping as he struggled to refocus.

The ship shuddered dramatically, the hull creaking and popping under the immense strain of the creature looming above them. It felt as though the very vessel was protesting against its demise, splinters of composite metal threatening to pierce the air as it fought to withstand the Kraken's weight.

"It's going to sink us!" Sonny shouted, his voice a mixture of fear and desperation, eyes wide with panic as he desperately clutched the ship's railing, bracing himself against the violent rocking.

Doyle, lying on the coarse deck and struggling to regain his breath, shot back with a cutting wit, "Oh, now you have plenty to say!" His voice dripped with sarcasm, a thin veneer of bravado concealing the sheer terror that coursed through them both as the battle for survival intensified.

Deborah returned to the deck, her staff in hand, feeling the weight of the moment. With a fierce determination, she slammed it onto the metal floor, and a brilliant blue light erupted from its tip, casting eerie shadows across the ship. An intense silence enveloped the scene, as if the very world held its breath. The massive Kraken, its dark tentacles reluctantly unclenching from the hull, began to sink back into the depths of the churning sea.

Turning her gaze toward the bridge, Deborah projected her voice with authority, shouting to The Driver, "Release the countermeasures, now!"

The Driver, a vigilant figure peering through the expansive front window of the bridge, turned sharply to the pilots. "Release the countermeasures!" he called out, urgency lacing his tone.

In response, multiple small flares shot out from both sides of the ship like shooting stars piercing the night sky, plunging into the inky waters below. The flares detonated with brilliant bursts, illuminating the depths momentarily as if the ocean itself had ignited. The Kraken, sensing the danger, recoiled further into the shadows, its monstrous form disappearing beneath the surface, leaving only ripples to mark its retreat.

Deborah raised her staff high, watching as the vibrant blue glow slowly faded into the dim twilight. With purposeful strides, she walked over to Doyle and offered her hand, concern etched on her face. "Are you okay?" she asked softly, her voice cutting through the charged atmosphere of the ship.

"Yes, I think I'm fine," Doyle responded, shaking off the remnants of their earlier ordeal. He turned his attention to the mast, where the sails were beginning to unfurl, creaking against the gentle sway of the ship. Just then, The Driver's voice crackled over the intercom, steady yet urgent. "We will be using the sails from here on out, as we have now entered Kraken-infested waters."

Doyle narrowed his eyes, glancing toward the bridge, his heart racing. "No shit!" he exclaimed, a mix of disbelief and adrenaline coursing through him as the gravity of the situation sank in.

"Sorry, everyone. That Kraken took us by surprise," The Driver announced over the intercom, his voice steady despite the choppy waters. "We're now just an hour away from the shallow waters near the island." He paused briefly, gauging the mood of the crew, before adding, "Kick back; it's going to be a smooth ride the rest of the way."

"Thank you, I really appreciate the update," Doyle responded, his voice strained as he wiped his face, still coughing up seawater from the last surge. He glanced around the deck, the saltiness of the sea air mixing with the tension in the atmosphere.

Deborah gently supported Doyle as they navigated toward one of the sturdy chairs that had, thankfully, withstood the chaos of the Kraken's attack. With care, she positioned the chair and helped him settle comfortably into it, ensuring he was secure. Meanwhile, Sonny busied himself gathering the scattered chairs knocked about by the wave, expertly maneuvering them back into a neat alignment along the deck, restoring order amid the turmoil.

The Driver, flanked by two diligent AI crew members, strolled purposefully along the beaten deck, keenly searching for any signs of damage. One crew member effortlessly scaled the towering main mast, gripping the metal rungs as he ascended to inspect the swaying cables high above.

The Driver turned to Doyle, concern etched on his face. "Are you doing alright, bud?" he asked, his voice tinged with a hint of worry.

"Yes, I'm good," Doyle responded, his eyes scanning the horizon. "Do you think there's a lot of damage?"

The Driver sighed and replied, "If there is, we'll take care of it while you guys are on the island searching for that crashed flying disk." His determination was evident, a mix of pragmatism and urgency in his tone.

"Doyle, everyone should return to their cabins, get dressed, and pack their gear. We'll be there soon," explained Deborah.

Doyle walked away, stretching his back. "I'm getting too old for flying through the air," he said, glancing back at Deborah. He turned the corner and descended the stairs to his cabin. Once inside, Eddie's lights flashed on. "Are you okay, sir?" the device inquired.

"Yes, Eddie, I'm fine. I need to put on some dry underwear," Doyle replied with a smile.

Doyle quickly stepped into the shower, the hot water cascading over him, refreshing him after a tough fight with a Kraken. Once he finished, he dried off briskly and dressed in a sturdy pair of military-style fatigues, the fabric rugged and worn from countless outings. He rummaged through his pack until he found his favorite floppy-billed hat, a familiar piece of gear that added a touch of personality to his otherwise practical outfit.

As he adjusted his hat, he turned to Eddie, the small robotic drone hovering nearby. "I need to check that I have enough cigars for this mission," he said with a playful wink, his demeanor lightening the mood.

Eddie, now fully charged and buzzing with energy, zipped through the air, responding with enthusiasm, "Yes, having plenty of cigars is definitely a good idea! They're essential for your downtime."

Doyle, flanked by Eddie, his trusty small drone hovering playfully at his side, stepped out of the cozy, rustic cabin and ascended the metal stairs to the expansive main deck of the ship. As he emerged into the fresh morning air, he noticed a stunning spectacle of the sun rising majestically over the horizon, painting the sky in vibrant shades of orange and pink that shimmered on the gently undulating sea. The ship had anchored four nautical miles from the island, its hull cradled by the inviting shallow waters that sparkled in the rising sunlight.

On the port side, Doyle spotted Sonny and Deborah, their figures leaning against the railing as they gazed out at the tranquil surroundings, the wind tousling their hair and the salt air invigorating their spirits.

"What's up, guys?" Doyle called out, making his way toward them, noticing a small pinnace bobbing lightly on the waves, its ladder lowered, beckoning toward the mysterious island awaiting their exploration.

"We're taking that charming little boat to the island. What about the Krakens?" Doyle asked, a mix of excitement and concern coloring his tone.

Deborah turned to him, her eyes twinkling with mischief as she replied, "These waters are too shallow for Krakens. If you look closely, you can see the fine grains of sand and colorful pebbles scattered across the sea floor, shimmering in the sunlight."

The AI crew members carefully lowered the team's equipment to the pinnace, their mechanical limbs moving with precision. As Deborah descended the sturdy ladder, her boots clanged softly against the metal rungs. She wore military-style fatigues that mirrored Doyle's, the fabric a faded olive green that spoke of countless missions. The only notable difference was the weapon at Doyle's side, a sleek 9mm handgun resting comfortably against his hip. At the same time, Deborah's unique choice of armament lay at her back, her staff poised and ready, a symbol of her combat readiness and skill. The air was thick with anticipation as they prepared to embark on their next challenge.

Sonny was the next to descend the creaking wooden ladder, each step deliberate and careful as he made his way down to the small boat swaying gently below. He donned a solid green outfit that clung to his frame, designed for both agility and durability, while a broad-brimmed brown hat shielded his face from the harsh sun, casting a shadow that obscured his determined eyes. At his hips, two imposing pistols rested in well-worn leather holsters, their polished barrels gleaming ominously, while a finely crafted Bowie knife, its blade reflecting the glimmers of sunlight, was sheathed across his chest, a silent promise of protection.

Once Sonny secured himself in the small boat, Doyle followed with a mix of trepidation and excitement bubbling within him. Eddie, a spirited companion with iridescent blades, flitted nervously near Doyle's head, his props producing a soft whir that added a lively energy to the tense atmosphere. Above them, a stout crew member grunted as he tugged on the ladder's rope, pulling it back up to the ship's deck with a satisfying clank that echoed over the lapping waves.

Deborah, leaning gracefully over the side of the boat, deftly worked the knot with agile fingers, her expression a blend of mischief and resolve. The sun caught the glint in her eyes as she finally freed the small boat from its tether, her voice cutting through the salty air with an invigorating confidence.

"We're off. No turning back now," Deborah declared to Doyle, her sly smile hinting at the thrill of the unknown adventure that awaited them beyond the horizon.

Sonny firmly grasped the oars, his muscles straining as he began to paddle rhythmically toward the distant shore, where soft golden sands awaited. In the back row, Doyle relaxed against the boat's edge, a mischievous grin spreading across his face as he reached into his pocket. He pulled out a cigar, its rich, earthy aroma wafting into the air, and lit it, the flame crackling gently against the backdrop of the rising sun. He turned back to watch the majestic ship they had just stepped off slowly recede, its massive silhouette becoming smaller and smaller against the sprawling sea. Beside him sat Deborah, her hair elegantly tied in a knot, exuding confidence. Dark sunglasses shielded her eyes as she gazed ahead, seemingly unfazed by the vastness of the water around them.

CHAPTER SEVEN

THE FORGOTTEN LAND

0745 HOURS
PRESENT-DAY
THE BAY OF EDWARD'S ISLAND

The Driver stands resolutely on the damaged deck of the ship, his eyes scanning the horizon as Deborah and her crew approach the rocky shores of Edward's Island. The sun glints off the dark blue waves, and the salty air fills his lungs, igniting a sense of purpose within him. He pivots, addressing his crew with a firm yet motivating tone. "Alright, team, time is of the essence. We've got limited time to get this ship seaworthy again. I want the welders to gather their tools and begin preparing for the mast repairs, ensuring everything is ready for a safe, sturdy fix.

Meanwhile, the divers should suit up and meticulously inspect the hull for any signs of damage below the waterline. Let's move swiftly and efficiently! We've got a challenging task ahead of us!" As he finishes, the crew springs into action, their energy amped as they prepare to tackle the repairs that lie ahead.

Deborah and Doyle nestled in the back of the pinnace, their gazes fixed on the shimmering expanse of water ahead as Sonny expertly wielded the paddles. The gentle undulations of the waves created a soothing rhythm. After a few moments, the small boat began to run aground, gently bumping against the sandy bottom of the beach.

With a determined expression, Sonny stepped out, the soft sand warming his feet as he pulled the boat ashore, water dripping from the metal hull. The rhythmic sound of tiny waves lapping at the coastline punctuated the tranquil scene. Doyle, eager to assist, followed suit, feeling the fine grains of sand shift beneath him.

Just then, Deborah's clear voice cut through the serenity. "We need to pack our gear into our backpacks and pull the boat up to those sturdy trees over there to secure it," she instructed, gesturing towards a cluster of tall, resilient palm trees that stood sentinel along the edge of the beach, their green needles glistening in the sunlight and swaying gently in the warm breeze. The air buzzed with the distant call of seabirds, creating a vivid backdrop for their important task ahead.

Deborah stepped out onto the soft, sun-warmed shoreline, the gentle waves lapping at her feet. She paused to take in the breathtaking view of the island's rugged mountains, their peaks crowned with lush vegetation that appeared almost vibrant against the clear azure sky. The air was filled with a salty tang, mingling with the earthy scent of the coastal flora.

As she walked, a low hum broke the tranquility, the unmistakable sound of Eddie, their companion drone, rising gracefully into the air beside her. With a polished, metallic frame that glinted in the sunlight, he hovered with precision, surveying the surroundings. "Ma'am," he reported, his voice steady yet imbued with urgency, "My radar and systems are operating at optimal levels. However, once we enter the dense jungle, my capabilities will become significantly limited. It would be prudent for me to remain here by the boat, where I can maintain open lines of communication with the ship and effectively track your movements throughout the expedition." His rotors whirred softly, a stark contrast to the landscape's serene beauty, underscoring the pivotal role he played in their adventure.

Deborah stood, her brow furrowed in thought as she processed the information that Eddie had just conveyed to her. "I believe you're right, Eddie," she said, her voice steady but laced with concern. "Communication will be nearly impossible in the dense jungle that lies ahead. Are you certain you can keep track of our movements?"

Eddie's lights blinked with a reassuring rhythm. "Yes, ma'am. I can monitor every movement of your pin devices, which I attached to each of your packs, via pings. However," he added, his tone shifting slightly, "If you venture underground, I will lose that signal completely." The weight of his warning hung in the air, a reminder of the challenges that awaited them in the uncharted wilderness.

A small, hidden door opened on Eddie's underbelly, revealing a sleek, shimmering compass nestled within. "Please take this compass," Eddie said, his voice resonating with a gentle urgency. "It's been carefully programmed to guide you back to my location. You will need it when you embark on your journey back to this very beach," he explained, his warm lights blinking as the sun glinted off the compass's polished surface.

Deborah carefully reached out and grasped the compass, its polished surface glinting in the dappled sunlight that filtered through the canopy above. "Thank you, Eddie," she said, her voice steady. "Stay close to the boat, but keep yourself out of sight. If any trouble arises, report it to The Driver; he will send help."

"Yes, ma'am," Eddie replied, his lights bright with determination. He soared back to the small boat, which sat gently against a tree. Sonny and Doyle had draped palm leaves over it, creating a makeshift camouflage that blended seamlessly with the lush surroundings. The air was alive with rustling leaves and distant birdsong, punctuating the tense atmosphere as Deborah prepared for what lay ahead.

"Alright, everyone. Sonny has meticulously analyzed the coordinates of the flying disk's last communication signal. By examining its speed and altitude at the time of transmission, he was able to calculate the most likely crash site," Deborah explained, her voice filled with urgency as she approached the two men who were poring over maps and equipment. The weight of their task hung over them as they prepared to embark on the search.

Eddie gracefully landed on a sturdy tree limb high above the small boat, shifting into low-energy mode. His lights flickered softly, casting an ethereal glow as he recharged his batteries. Below, Sonny led the group along a gentle incline that meandered through a landscape scattered with imposing boulders and ancient trees, their gnarled branches stretching majestically into the clouds like nature's guardians.

Deborah followed closely, her eyes wide with wonder at the vibrant foliage surrounding them, while Doyle trailed behind, his steps heavy with the weight of their ascent. As they climbed further from the cool embrace of the beach, the air grew thick and stifling, the humidity enveloping them like a warm blanket.

"Wow, it's getting hot," Doyle exclaimed, a sheen of sweat glistening on his forehead as it trickled down the side of his face, a reminder of the increasing warmth that pressed in around them.

"Big difference from the tundra of Antarctica," Deborah said, smiling back at him.

Doyle wiped the perspiration from his brow, feeling the oppressive heat of the sun pressing down like an unwelcome weight. "You're absolutely right about that," he replied, his voice a mix of exhaustion and vigilance as he looked up at the immense, ancient trees that loomed overhead, their branches stretching out like giant arms reaching for the sky.

Sonny, ever the vigilant scout, pressed forward, his keen eyes darting through the tangled underbrush and shadowy thickets, searching for any signs of potential danger. He intermittently halted, standing perfectly still to absorb the forest's sounds, the rustle of leaves, the distant call of a bird, and the faint buzzing of insects. In these moments of stillness, he took a deep, calming breath, filling his lungs with the thick, humid air that clung to him like a damp shroud. Under the lush canopy, his vibrant blue skin shimmered, a striking contrast to the verdant tapestry of foliage and earthy tones surrounding him, heightening his otherworldly presence in this wild, untamed landscape.

As they ambled along a narrow, rocky ledge that jutted out high above a winding river below, the sun cast a warm, golden hue on everything it touched. Doyle's eyes beheld a magnificent sight: enormous, prehistoric creatures gathered by the water's edge, their massive bodies silhouetted against the shimmering surface of the lazy river. The gentle sounds of water flowing over smooth stones created a serene backdrop to this breathtaking scene.

"What kind of animals are those?" Doyle asked, his voice awed as he pointed toward the graceful giants.

Deborah glanced down, her eyes sparkling with excitement as she observed the magnificent beings. "Those are what you would call dinosaurs," she replied, a smile blooming on her lips, brightening her face with wonder.

"Dinosaurs? Really?" Doyle's expression was a mixture of disbelief and astonishment, his mind racing to grasp the reality of what he was witnessing.

With a soft, melodic laugh that intertwined with the rustling leaves overhead, Deborah reassured him, "Yes, really." Her gaze remained fixed on the remarkable creatures, their presence evoking a sense of wonder that seemed to transcend time and space.

Doyle removed his weathered hat and dabbed the sweat from his forehead, feeling the heat of the sun bear down on him. He glanced at Deborah, a hint of concern in his eyes. "Are they dangerous?" he asked, his voice tinged with apprehension.

Deborah stepped closer, her hand reassuringly patting him on the back. "Sometimes," she replied cautiously, her gaze following Sonny as he rounded a bend in the narrow trail, momentarily disappearing. "But we can't linger here. We need to keep moving," she urged, her tone both firm and encouraging, as the sounds of the wilderness enveloped them.

The group forged ahead toward the crash site, their boots crunching on the gravelly path that meandered through thick underbrush. As they descended into a verdant valley, the vibrant hues of wildflowers and lush ferns enveloped them, and the crisp, clean scent of damp earth filled the air. After a brief descent, the trail began its ascent, eventually leading them to the glistening river that Doyle had glimpsed earlier, where several large animals had disturbed the area's tranquility.

"This looks like the perfect place to take a breather," Sonny declared, his voice echoing slightly in the open space. With a decisive thud, he dropped his heavy backpack onto a sun-soaked, flat boulder that jutted prominently at the riverbank, the stone warm beneath his fingers and speckled with patches of soft green moss.

Doyle took off his pack and began to sift through its contents until he uncovered the sandwich lovingly prepared by the ship's crew the night before. He examined it for a moment, noting the fresh ingredients and careful wrapping, before taking a big, satisfying bite. "I've encountered my fair share of dense brush in the past, but I think this might take the cake," he said, his voice slightly muffled by the sandwich. As he chewed, the flavors burst to life, harmonizing perfectly with the melodic chorus of chirping birds and the soothing rush of the river flowing just a few feet away.

The group sat in a sunlit clearing, the warm glow filtering through the leaves above as they leisurely enjoyed their lunch. Silence filled the air until they were suddenly interrupted by the faint but unmistakable sound of footsteps approaching from behind. "Everyone, grab your packs and hide," Sonny instructed, his voice low and urgent, eyes scanning the surroundings for potential danger.

Doyle and Deborah sprang into action, ducking behind the thick foliage to the left of the winding trail, their hearts pounding with a mix of excitement and trepidation. Sonny, quick on his feet, slipped behind a large, moss-covered boulder to the right, his breath held and senses heightened as he blended into the shadows.

As they crouched in silence, the atmosphere felt electric, charged with anticipation. Deborah, her curiosity getting the better of her, cautiously peered around the trunk of an ancient tree. To her utter astonishment, she spotted a tiny fairy walking along the trail like a sunbeam brought to life. He was no taller than her hand, with iridescent wings that sparkled like dewdrops in the morning light.

The little man wore snug jeans that hugged his small frame and a whimsical hat perched jauntily atop his head. A tousled mane of hair framed his delicate features, and he hummed a cheerful melody, blissfully unaware of the wide-eyed watchers hidden in the underbrush. Each step he took seemed to dance upon the earthy ground, spreading an air of magic and wonder through the tranquil forest.

Deborah, her staff in hand and determination in her eyes, emerged from the shadows of the ancient tree, the dappled sunlight filtering through the leaves above. "Halt! Who goes there?" She called out, her voice firm and resonant, directed at the diminutive figure before her.

The tiny man, a fairy with delicate wings shimmering like gossamer in the light, froze in place, his heart racing at the sight of the imposing figure. He quickly raised his hands in a gesture of peace. "It's just me," he stammered, his voice trembling with a mixture of fear and recognition.

Deborah, unwavering, pointed her staff at him, the tip glowing faintly. "Who is 'me?'" she demanded, her brow furrowed with suspicion.

As the fairy squinted up at her, relief washed over his features. A smile broke through his initial fright as he realized who stood before him. "Deborah! It's me, Tom Little," he exclaimed, his eyes twinkling with familiarity and joy.

Deborah lowered her staff, a glimmer of curiosity in her eyes. "Tom, what brings you to this remote island? It seems a bit far from home, don't you think?"

"Oh, yes, ma'am," Tom, the tiny fairy with iridescent wings, replied enthusiastically. "I'm here hunting for mushrooms. They're in season right now, you know. The forest is bursting with them!"

Doyle cautiously stepped out from behind a cluster of vibrant ferns and made his way toward Deborah. He felt a mixture of curiosity and apprehension as Tom looked him over with a smile. "So, is this the human who destroyed the tunnel?" he asked, his voice lighthearted yet inquisitive.

Deborah wrapped her arm around Doyle's shoulder, a protective gesture. "Yes, he's the one," she declared proudly. "And he is my husband."

"I'm not... ouch, that hurts," Doyle started to protest, feeling the gentle pinch of Deborah's fingers as she clutched his shoulder.

"Just go with it," she whispered urgently, her eyes pleading as she encouraged him to play along.

Tom, shifting his gaze between the two of them, raised an eyebrow. "Husband, huh? Well, I was going to mention that my friend Fred is still single," he added, a mischievous grin spreading across his tiny face. "But I see you don't need a new man in your life!"

With that, the lighthearted banter hung in the air, weaving a moment of camaraderie among the unlikely trio amidst the enchanting backdrop of the island's vibrant wilderness.

Sonny emerged from behind the massive boulder, its rocky surface warmed by the early morning sun. "Morning, Tom," he called out, his voice filled with a sense of adventure as he greeted the fairy, whose iridescent wings glistened with the first light of day.

Tom turned to face him, a broad smile spreading across his delicate features, his eyes twinkling with the knowledge of hidden secrets. "Sonny! I had a feeling you wouldn't be far behind. Let me guess, you're on a quest to find that flying disk that came crashing down a few days ago?"

"That's right," Deborah replied, her eyes bright with anticipation. "Did you happen to witness its fall?"

Tom lifted off the ground with a gentle flutter, his wings beating rhythmically like the soft rustle of leaves in a breeze. "I didn't see it crash; I witnessed it when it was shot down. My cousin and I were diligently farming mushrooms on the lush slopes of the Cedar Tree

Hills when we heard the roar of its engine above us. In a split second, a cave troll, a hulking creature with jagged teeth and a menacing look, fired a laser weapon at the disk, striking it with a blinding flash and sending it spiraling down into the thick underbrush of the hills."

"Cave trolls?" Doyle echoed, his eyebrow arched in disbelief. He turned slightly. "Why wouldn't there be cave trolls? After all, we are having a conversation with a fairy," he said to himself.

Sonny glanced at Deborah, his brow furrowed with concern. "Cedar Tree Hills isn't all that far away," he reassured her, his voice steady.

Deborah gave a slight nod of acknowledgment before turning her attention to Tom. "You and your cousin need to leave this island as soon as possible," she urged, her tone serious.

Tom responded earnestly, "We have our boat packed to the brim with supplies and ready to set sail. I was just searching for a lucky rock to take home to my son," he explained, a hint of wistfulness in his voice.

"Where's your boat?" Deborah inquired, her eyes scanning the river.

Tom pointed enthusiastically with one of his tiny fingers, his expression brightening. "She's over yonder," he said, directing their gaze toward the river.

The group turned to look, and there, a small barge bobbed gently on the water, heavily laden with an assortment of mushrooms, their earthy tones contrasting with the vibrant greens of the surrounding foliage. Perched atop the mound of mushrooms was a chubby fairy with cheeks rosy and round. "Hi!" the chubby fairy called out cheerfully to everyone with a voice ringing with light-hearted joy that cut through the tension in the air.

"Tom, you and your cousin cannot possibly float that barge down the river and out to sea. The animals would surely devour you like a morsel," Deborah implored, her voice quivering with concern as she gazed at the glimmering waters, which danced with sunlight and concealed lurking dangers beneath the surface.

Tom the fairy let out a light-hearted laugh, his wings shimmering in the golden light. "Oh, we're not embarking on the river journey you envision. We're utilizing the secret underground stream, a hidden channel so narrow and winding that only fairies can traverse it. It flows through the ancient roots of the forest and leads us directly to our magical home, a sanctuary filled with vibrant flora and fairy lights."

Deborah's face lit up with a warm smile, her eyes sparkling with mischief. "I should have known you'd have a safe route home all figured out."

Tom tipped his well-worn hat back on his head, a playful glint in his eye. "I shall be on my way then. Just be cautious on your travels through the treacherous lava fields that lie between here and the impressive Cedar Tree Hills." After offering them his best wishes, he gracefully took flight, gliding effortlessly over to the sturdy little barge. The gentle creaking of its wooden frame echoed in the stillness as he raised the anchor, and Deborah and Doyle watched, captivated, as the barge slipped quietly out of sight, its silhouette gradually swallowed by a bend in the glistening river.

Sonny adjusted the heavy pack on his broad shoulders, its straps digging slightly into his skin. “We need to get moving,” he urged, glancing at the distant horizon where the sun was directly overhead.

“Roger that,” Doyle replied with an amused grin. He swiftly grabbed Deborah’s pack, the fabric worn but well cared for, and handed it to her with a flourish. Then, with an eyebrow raised in curiosity, he posed a question. “Why did you tell Tom I was your husband?”

Deborah let out a resigned sigh, her expression shifting to one of frustration as she tucked a stray lock of hair behind her ear. “You heard him; he’s always trying to play matchmaker, constantly pushing me toward Fred. And let’s be real, Fred only has his eyes on me for a chance to get naked pictures of me that he wants to share with Tom. Those fairies are really a perverted bunch.”

Doyle couldn’t help but chuckle, the sound rich and warm. “You calling anyone perverted is just too funny, you know that?”

“I’m only perverted for you, darling,” Deborah retorted, her laughter ringing out like a harmonious melody, intertwining with the gentle rustle of leaves in the breeze as they prepared to embark on the next leg of their adventure.

They discovered a location along the river where a cluster of smooth, sunlit rocks formed a natural barrier, creating a gentle waterfall that cascaded into a shallow pool. This spot offered an ideal place to cross without getting swept away. Afterward, they navigated through the tangled undergrowth, carefully hacking away at the thick brush until they finally emerged onto a narrow gravel trail that wound its way away from the riverbank.

After several more hours of navigating the rugged terrain, they finally reached a stark, desolate expanse, the infamous lava fields. This eerily beautiful landscape, covered with hardened lava, is cracked and twisted into bizarre formations. "Welcome to the lava fields," Sonny declared, his tone a blend of respect and wariness as he gestured to the eerie vista stretching before them.

Sensing the weight of the surroundings, Deborah instinctively unfastened her sturdy staff, a well-worn piece embossed with intricate carvings. With her heart racing, she tightened her grip on it, allowing its familiar texture to ground her. Doyle noticed her sudden shift in demeanor and, with a hint of concern in his voice, asked, "Are you expecting trouble?"

Deborah's eyes narrowed as she scanned the rugged landscape, her gaze settling on the peculiar, honeycomb-like rock formations riddled throughout the area. "These fields are a known habitat for what we call lava-beasts," she explained, her voice steady yet cautious. "The porous rocks provide perfect dens for these small, nimble, four-legged creatures. They're not just curious; they can be quite mischievous and territorial if you inadvertently cross into their lair." Her words resonated in the heavy silence, the ominous beauty of the lava fields enveloping them as they moved deeper into the mysterious terrain.

Sonny paused in his tracks, casting a glance back at Deborah and Doyle as they trudged to catch up. "We should form a tight line as we walk," he suggested, his voice steady yet filled with urgency. "It will make us seem larger to any predators we encounter, and hopefully, the lions will think twice before attacking."

Doyle furrowed his brow, puzzled. "So, the lava beasts are actually lions?"

Deborah turned to Doyle, shaking her head slightly. "They may resemble lions, but they belong to a different classification altogether. They aren't part of the canine family at all." She continued, her expression serious. "These creatures can leap great distances like lions, and they possess exceptionally long claws that make them formidable hunters."

As they ventured deeper into the treacherous lava fields, the molten landscape twisted and shimmered with heat, casting an eerie glow. Suddenly, two massive, lion-like creatures emerged from the shadows, their muscular bodies rippling with power, and deep growls reverberated from their throats. "I'm really not comfortable with this, Deborah," Sonny whispered, his eyes wide with apprehension, as he drew both of his pistols.

"Do not shoot them!" Deborah commanded, as she tightened her grip around the smooth, polished staff, feeling its familiar weight in her hands. She raised it high above her head, her voice low and steady as she began to chant an ancient incantation. A brilliant light emanated from the staff, illuminating the darkened surroundings and momentarily piercing through the oppressive air. The lava beasts, their fierce eyes glinting with suspicion, hesitated but did not retreat; instead, they hissed ominously as the trio moved cautiously past them.

"Do not make a sound. Just keep walking," Deborah instructed firmly, her voice steady, yet laced with urgency. Each step felt like a fragile dance between danger and resolve, the weight of the moment hanging heavily in the air.

Once they exited the sulfurous expanse of the lava fields, the lush jungle enveloped them once more. Towering in the distance, the ancient cedar trees of the Cedar Tree Hills stood majestically, their lofty branches reaching toward the clouds like the fingers of giants. Deborah tightened her grip on her staff and secured it on her back before turning to Doyle with a reassuring expression. "The lava beast will not venture beyond that area in pursuit of us. We are safe from their wrath now."

"That's a relief," Doyle replied, glancing back in the direction they had come. "They definitely seemed less than pleased with our presence."

Sonny, ever the planner, chimed in as they pressed deeper into the jungle. "Once we cross into the Cedar Tree Hills, the thick canopy will almost completely obscure the sunlight. I can only hope the Disk is resting on the forest floor rather than hanging high among the branches, far out of reach."

They continued their trek for another half-hour, the sounds of the jungle growing louder around them with each step. Finally, they reached the towering cedars. As they entered this new realm, the brilliance of the day faded into twilight, the dense foliage creating an almost surreal darkness that felt heavy and alive. Shadows danced among the ancient trunks, heightening their sense of adventure and the mystery that lay before them.

CHAPTER EIGHT

THE CRASH SITE

1638 HOURS
PRESENT-DAY
THE CEDAR TREE HILLS, EDWARD'S ISLAND

The trees of the Cedar Tree Hills shed millions of needles, creating a thick, blanket-like layer of soft, fragrant cedar that muffles footsteps and fills the air with a rich, woody aroma. Above, the majestic cedar trees stretch skyward, their massive trunks encased in rough, dark bark. At the same time, their expansive, lush canopies filter sunlight, casting intricate dappled shade across the forest floor. It feels as though one has stepped into a timeless realm on Edward's island, where the essence of magic thrives in every breath.

Scattered among the towering trees are charming little huts, each crafted from weathered wood and woven with vines, their rounded roofs resembling the forest's natural formations. These whimsical structures blend harmoniously with their surroundings, as if they were part of the landscape itself.

"What are those little huts?" Doyle asks, his eyes wide with curiosity as he surveys the scene, captivated by the allure of the hidden world.

"They belong to a secretive race of dwarfs," Deborah replies, her voice hushed with reverence. "These small people are incredibly private, choosing to remain hidden from prying eyes. Their huts are intricately connected by a labyrinthine tunnel system that snakes beneath the towering cedar roots, enabling them to move quietly and unseen throughout their enchanted territory."

The group meanders through the tranquil forest, where towering cedar trees stretch their enormous branches high above, creating a cathedral-like atmosphere bathed in mottled sunlight. Sonny, with his vigilant gaze, scans the underbrush and canopy, searching for any signs of the crashed flying disk. As they venture deeper into the secluded area, he notices the damage to the majestic cedars: their bark stripped away, dark scorch marks marring their vibrant green foliage, hinting at the violent encounter that occurred just days before.

Finally, Sonny's heart skips a beat as he spots the disk, a grotesque amalgamation of twisted metal and shattered components, hanging precariously about twenty feet off the ground, ensnared in the grasp of a massive tree. The wreckage dangles ominously, its surface glinting erratically in the sunlight, revealing burn patterns that speak to a catastrophic failure.

"Wow, it looks like a heat-seeking missile struck the disk," Doyle remarks, his tone a mixture of awe and disbelief as he tilts his head back, scanning the damaged craft with wide eyes.

"A laser weapon," Sonny counters, his voice steady and analytical as he studies the wreckage in detail, noting the precision of the charred edges that tell a more calculated story of destruction.

Deborah, a few paces away, squints up at the wreck with a determined expression, her brow furrowed in concentration. "Doyle, climb up there and see if the pilots are inside," she instructs firmly, her voice carrying a sense of urgency that cuts through the forest's stillness.

"Roger that," Doyle replies, excitement flickering in his eyes as he drops his backpack with a thud onto the soft earth. He swiftly pulls out his climbing gear, the metallic clinks of carabiners echoing as he prepares for the ascent. He expertly tosses a heavy rope with a robust hook, watching as it sails and securely wraps around a sturdy limb near the wreckage.

Taking a deep breath, he begins to ascend the thick, frayed rope, his feet pressing firmly against the rugged bark of the ancient cedar tree. The gnarled texture beneath his soles offers a reassuring grip, each fibrous ridge anchoring him as he climbs higher. With every upward pull, the anticipation thickens like the humid air around him, drawing him irresistibly closer to the wreckage that hangs precariously from a splintered limb above. He pauses, taking in the mangled craft, its once-sleek surface marred by deep fissures and blackened patches, bearing the scars of a violent plunge. The air buzzes with an electric tension as he steels himself, ready to unearth the mysteries entwined within its charred and battered remains.

Doyle carefully traverses through the gaping hole on the side of the disk, the acrid scent of burnt metal and scorched wood swirling around him like a ghostly shroud. Each step is deliberate as he navigates toward the heart of the craft, his senses heightened, aware of the eerie silence enveloping him. The doorway to the cockpit area, where a mysterious, glimmering liquid once pooled, has been consumed by flames, leaving only a jagged void. Upon entering the main cabin, he lifts his gaze to the cockpit, searching for any traces of the pilots. The cockpit, once bustling with activity and life, now stands empty, shrouded in shadows that amplify the unsettling feeling that clings to him as he realizes he is utterly alone in this forsaken vessel.

Doyle navigated carefully toward the narrow opening on the disk's side, his senses heightened by the eerie stillness around him. Leaning over the edge, he peered outside, scanning the scene below. He looked at Deborah with a serious expression, saying, "There's no one here, and no indications that anyone has entered this place since the wreck."

As if on cue, Sonny made his way back to Deborah's side, his eyes sharp from scrutinizing the area for any signs of life. The tension in the air was thick. "Ma'am," he reported, his voice calm yet urgent, "The pilots didn't leave the craft on foot. According to the evidence I found, it looks like they were carried away by two individuals, possibly cave trolls, heading off in that direction," he said, pointing towards a thicket of trees shrouded in shadows. "As for the two officers, they appear to have been escorted in the opposite direction by a solitary figure, who also shows traits of being a cave troll." His gaze drifted back to the wreck, where the remnants of the incident loomed ominously, a reminder of the chaos that had unfolded. The gravity of their findings settled heavily between them, thickening the air with uncertainty.

Deborah lifted her gaze to meet Doyle's, a fierce determination etched across her features. "We need to plant the explosives inside the disk to obliterate the electronics. That technology is far too dangerous to fall into the hands of those who would exploit it."

"Understood," Doyle replied, his voice calm and resolute. He turned back to the disordered interior of the battered disk, meticulously examining the jumble of wires and fragile circuitry. He mentally mapped out where to place the charges for maximum effect.

"Sonny," Deborah continued, her voice steady but laced with urgency, "focus on locating the pilots since they're not in the wreckage; they likely perished in the crash. Reports suggest that the remaining officers now reside in Edwards compound, which lies directly along the route they exited." She cast a wary glance toward the distant horizon, her mind racing with the stakes of their next move as the weight of their mission pressed heavily upon her.

Doyle carefully lowered himself down the rope, feeling the rough fibers against his hands as he descended. With a soft thud, he landed on the ground, his heart racing slightly from the adrenaline of the task. "All the explosives are set and ready to be detonated," he informed Deborah, his voice steady despite the tension in the air.

"Thanks," she replied, a flicker of relief crossing her features as she took stock of their surroundings, her senses alert for any signs of danger.

"Over here!" Sonny called out, his urgency punctuating the stillness around them. Doyle and Deborah hastened to his side, their footsteps muffled by the needles beneath them. As they approached, the scene unfolded before them: the remains of the two AI pilots lay scattered across the ground in a grotesque display. Fragments of metal glinted dully in the fading light, while wires, some severed and frayed, snaked out like discarded tendrils from the lifeless forms. Computer chips, once vital pieces of machinery, were scattered haphazardly, adding to the disarray.

"It looks like they dumped them here after removing them from the disk," Sonny explained, gesturing to the chaotic scene with a furrowed brow. The air hung heavy with the metallic scent of technology, and the weight of their mission pressed down on them, a constant reminder of the stakes involved.

"From the looks of it, the Dwarves have eagerly scavenged the mangled remains of these advanced machines for any useful components," Sonny observed, gesturing toward the scattered debris that lay strewn across the forest floor like the aftermath of a fierce storm. Jagged shards of metal and twisted wires glinted ominously in the dappled sunlight. "Or perhaps someone wants us to believe that's the case," Deborah countered, her expression thoughtful as she ran a hand through her hair, a sign of her unease. "The Dwarves have little need for electrical parts; they tend to favor robust, natural materials that enhance their exceptional craftsmanship."

Sonny turned to Deborah, a flicker of frustration crossing his features. "Should I burn these remnants?"

"No. The leftover parts of these AI pilots are practically worthless now," Deborah replied, her gaze shifting toward the faintly illuminated path that led into the depths of the woods. It seemed almost ominous, hinting at the uncertainty of what lay ahead. She squared her shoulders, determination setting her jaw. "We must act swiftly to locate our officers, as every moment counts. I have a strong belief that just beyond this thick, towering cedar forest lies Edward, strategically positioned and poised for action. He may be ready to confront us or, more likely, to direct us into the concealed traps he has meticulously set along our path."

Sonny strides forward with purpose, taking the lead as the group navigates through the lush, towering trees of the forest. They head toward the spot where the two officers were led from the chaotic crash site by their captors. Once they are a safe distance from the ominously suspended metal disk, Doyle grips the detonator tightly, his heart racing with anticipation. With a decisive press, he activates the device, and a series of sharp, muffled pops echo through the stillness of the woods. The sound suddenly pierces the serene atmosphere, as wisps of acrid smoke curl from the disk. With a heavy thud, the now charred and smoldering relic crashes down onto the soft loam of the forest floor, scattering needles and twigs in its wake.

Deborah turns to Doyle, her eyes glinting with determination. "Once I've confirmed that it's safe," she says with conviction, "I'll dispatch a specialized team of AI rangers to clear away all this wreckage meticulously. We're dedicated to restoring Cedar Tree Hills to its former glory, ensuring that the natural beauty of this area stays the same." With her words, a vision of renewal fills the air, hinting at a brighter, revitalized future amidst the remnants of disaster.

As they crest the steep exit from the Cedar Tree Hills, the sun sinks lower, splashing the sky with hues of orange and purple. The crisp mountain air fills their lungs, carrying the scent of cedar and damp earth. Sonny comes to an abrupt halt, his keen eyes scanning the rugged terrain as shadows lengthen. "Nightfall will soon embrace us," he announces with a sense of urgency. "We should establish our camp here, nestled beneath the sprawling canopy of the ancient cedar trees. Their large trunks and fragrant needles will provide us with much-needed protection from the encroaching chill and the unseen dangers of the night. Traveling in darkness in this treacherous mountain region could prove catastrophic."

"I wholeheartedly agree. The inky darkness of nightfall only serves to empower Edward and his formidable band of cave trolls. The Cedar Tree Hills, with their sprawling, verdant landscape, conceal intricate underground tunnels meticulously guarded by the dwarves. This enchanted area is teeming with life and enchantment, offering safety to those who belong. Beyond its borders, however, lies a stark and imposing terrain where rugged granite cliffs loom like ancient sentinels over the land. In this unforgiving expanse, the trolls have carved out their own shadowy network of passageways, maneuvering through the depths with stealth and cunning, waiting to strike at the slightest provocation under the cover of night."

Sonny and Doyle set to work establishing their campsite, the air filled with the earthy scent of cedar needles. Meanwhile, Deborah knelt on the forest floor, meticulously arranging stones into a sturdy circle for the fire and collecting dry twigs and branches to fuel the flames.

"Doyle, once we have the camp set up, I need you to scale that towering cedar tree and try to get in touch with Eddie," Deborah instructed, her eyes sparkling with unwavering determination as she surveyed the dense forest surrounding them.

"Absolutely, I've got it covered," Doyle replied confidently, his gaze fixed on the massive tree. "What's the best way to climb this giant?" he asked, steadying his tone as he assessed its considerable height and gnarled branches.

Sonny rummaged through his meticulously organized hiking pack, his fingers brushing against the familiar gear until he retrieved a compact cable pulley system. He then glanced up at the magnificent cedar tree looming overhead, its grand stature reminiscent of a timeless sentinel, its robust limbs stretching skyward as if reaching for the clouds. "This tree must be over eight hundred feet tall," he remarked, a tone of deep admiration threading through his voice.

With the confidence of someone well-versed in outdoor adventures, he deftly unclipped a compact drone securely affixed to the side of his pack and attached the cable. "The drone will install a pulley high in the branches of the tree," Sonny explained to Doyle, his eyes sparkling with excitement. "This will allow you to pull yourself up using the cable. I have about one thousand feet of cable available, so when we double it up, it can elevate you five hundred feet into the tree," he added, ensuring Doyle understood that he would have to climb the rest of the way.

With a soft whirr, the drone powered on, effortlessly lifting the cable into the air. It ascended out of sight, vanishing into the lush green canopy overhead, and quickly returned after successfully securing the pulley to a section of the trunk and threading the cable through it. With the pulley in place, Sonny grasped the loose end of the cable, carefully packed the drone back into its case, and then handed Doyle his harness. As Doyle donned the gear, Sonny moved with practiced precision to attach the cable. He meticulously checked every connection, ensuring that Doyle was securely fastened and ready to tackle the challenging ascent ahead. The air was thick with anticipation, and the sound of distant winds added to the sense of adventure that permeated the moment.

Doyle tightened his grip on the sturdy cable, feeling the rough texture of its coarse fibers press into his gloves as he began his ascent up the venerable cedar tree. Its bark, thick and weathered, bore the scars of decades of ferocious storms, telling silent tales of endurance and strength. He skillfully navigated from one limb to the next, each movement sending a cascade of fragrant needles rustling around him, their vibrant green hue creating a striking contrast against the deep, rich brown of the trunk.

When he finally reached the pulley, he paused, allowing himself a moment to relish the breathtaking view that unfolded before him. With meticulous care, he secured the cable, ensuring it would hold firm against the elements. Bolstered by determination, he pressed on, pushing through the thick canopy. As he breached the lush foliage, a stunning panorama revealed itself, filling his senses with wonder and igniting a sense of adventure that spurred him onward.

To the west, the sun dipped low on the horizon, painting the sky in shades of orange, pink, and lavender as it gradually sank into the water. Doyle could see a large compound that stood out, its silhouette stark against the colorful canvas of dusk. "That must be Edward's compound," he thought, feeling the weight of his mission pressing heavily on his mind. He turned north and saw their massive ship anchored in the bay. He reached into his pocket and pulled out a compact radio earpiece; the cool plastic felt reassuring as he prepared to communicate his next move.

"How about you, Eddie? Come in," Doyle called into the radio, his voice cutting through the thick, damp air above the forest.

From its perch high in the branches of a sturdy tree, the small drone's lights flickered in response, illuminating the shadowy undergrowth below. "I hear you, Doyle," Eddie replied, his tone clear and steady.

"Eddie, is this a secure transmission?" Doyle asked, his eyes scanning the dense treetops for any sign of movement.

"Yes," Eddie confirmed. "It is scrambled and difficult to break the code so that we can speak freely without fear of interception."

A smile crept across Doyle's face, relieved by the assurance. "You are the best, Eddie. We have located the wreckage of the downed flying disk, along with the two pilots who perished in the crash. However, we haven't yet found the two officers, and the daylight is fading fast. We're setting up camp for the night. Could you relay that information to The Driver?" he requested, knowing the urgency of their situation.

"Good job, sir," Eddie responded with a hint of admiration. "Yes, I will pass that message along. I have also pinpointed your exact location; I lost your signal for the last few hours due to the heavy canopy above."

"Yeah, it's been tough," Doyle admitted, glancing at the thick canopy, now below him, that had blocked out much of the sunlight all day. "We've been completely shielded at the crash site. I had to climb a tree to reach you. You'll lose our location again until sunrise, when we plan to move out," he explained, his voice steady despite the uncertainty of their circumstances.

"I understand. Wishing you a restful night, Doyle," Eddie replied, the small drone's lights dimming slightly as it settled in for the evening, ready to support Doyle through the dark hours ahead.

As the campfire flames flickered and danced in the cool evening air, Deborah and Sonny sat wrapped in their jackets, enjoying the warmth and the tranquil sounds of the night. Suddenly, they noticed Doyle gracefully gliding down from the treetop, his movements smooth and deliberate. He unhooked the cable and removed his harness with practiced ease.

"Wow, the view from up there was absolutely stunning," Doyle said, taking a moment to catch his breath. "I could see the entire island spread out beneath me. There's a compound a few miles to the west that I spotted."

Deborah nodded knowingly, her expression turning serious. "Yes, that's Edwards' compound. He typically uses it for his drug operations," she replied, her voice low and cautious. The weight of their situation hung in the air, mingling with the crackling of the fire.

Doyle strolled over to the warm glow of the campfire, the flickering flames casting dancing shadows on his face. He kicked off his dusty boots and settled down comfortably on his side, propping his head up on one hand. "So, who's going to share the first ghost story?" he inquired, a mischievous grin spreading across his face.

Deborah let out a soft, melodic laugh that rippled through the cool night air. "If I told you any of my ghost stories, trust me, you wouldn't get a wink of sleep for an entire week," she replied, her eyes sparkling with intrigue.

Doyle nodded thoughtfully, the firelight reflecting a mixture of curiosity and caution in his gaze. "Yeah, I can believe that. Never mind, though; let's shift gears and talk about something else," he suggested, looking around at the serene surroundings, eager to explore a different topic.

Meanwhile, back on the ship anchored at a safe distance from the rugged shores of Edwards Island, The Driver walked along the deck, inspecting the extensive repairs that had occupied the crew throughout the day. The salty breeze rustled through the rigging as the sun dipped low on the horizon, casting a warm golden glow over the vessel.

Approaching him was the highest-ranking crew member, a seasoned AI sailor with sharp eyes. "Sir," he began with a respectful nod, "I'm pleased to report that we've completed the repairs on the main mast and completed the underwater hull inspections. I can confirm that there is no damage to the hull after our thorough examination."

The Driver paused to absorb the information, nodding in approval. "Thank you for your diligence," he replied, his voice steady and commanding. "Please ensure that your crew continues anchoring operations tonight with double the teams for night watch. I have just received word that we will be remaining here overnight to ensure our readiness for any unforeseen circumstances."

"Yes, sir, Captain," the crew member responded, a note of determination in his tone, before turning sharply and striding back to relay the orders to the rest of the crew. Their preparations reflected the disciplined nature of life at sea.

The Driver sauntered to the ship's railing, staring across the shimmering bay at the island's outline in the darkness. "I'd much rather be out there with them, enjoying the freedom of the land, than trapped here on this vessel," he murmured to himself. Just then, a group of large, unfamiliar prehistoric birds glided past, their massive wings casting fleeting shadows on the water's surface, as a large full moon rose above the horizon.

As the thick darkness enveloped the campsite, the campfire flickered fiercely, casting a warm, golden glow that danced across the surrounding shadows. Doyle and Deborah huddled closely around the crackling fire, their faces illuminated by the flickering flames. The sound of the burning wood popped and crackled, mingling with the distant rustling of needles stirred by a gentle breeze. Sonny had earlier departed, his broad, rugged form blending into the darkness of the nearby trees as he sought a meal in the dense underbrush.

"How much of a fight do you think Edward will put up?" Doyle asked, his voice low and tense as he fixed his gaze on the lively flames, lost in thought.

Deborah leaned back against a fallen log, her expression difficult to read in the dim light. "He's not much of a fighter himself," she replied, her voice steady yet laced with resolve, "but the cave trolls he recruits for his drug trade are formidable. They are fierce and relentless, with a reputation for brutality."

"What's your plan to rescue the officers?" Doyle queried, concern etched on his brow as he shifted his focus to her.

Deborah shook her head slowly, a mixture of determination and frustration flickering across her features. "It's hard to say. If they're still alive, Edward will likely use them as pawns to manipulate us, playing our emotions like a master puppeteer. If they're not, then we'll have to show no mercy in eradicating Edward and his entire clan."

"Wow, that's pretty harsh," Doyle replied, taken aback by the intensity of her convictions.

"He deserves whatever fury I unleash upon him," Deborah snapped, her eyes flashing with fierce determination, revealing the deep-seated rage she felt towards their adversary.

Just then, Sonny emerged from the thick underbrush, his presence commanding as he returned to camp with a broad, triumphant smile illuminating his face. In his hand, he proudly displayed a string of shimmering fish, their scales catching the firelight like precious gems. The campfire flickered against his weathered features, highlighting the satisfaction of a successful hunt.

"What do you have there?" Doyle asked, curiosity piqued as he leaned forward to get a better look at Sonny's catch.

"These are a type of perch I caught from a nearby stream, just beyond the Cedar Tree Hills," Sonny explained, holding up the vibrant fish for inspection. Their scales glistened brilliantly in the warm glow of the fire, a testament to Sonny's skill and resourcefulness in the wild.

The small group of unlikely warriors gathered around a crackling campfire, preparing fish Sonny had caught for a hearty feast. The scent of the fresh fish, seasoned with wild herbs collected earlier, filled the air, promising a satisfying meal after a long day. Deborah, their determined leader with fierce eyes and a commanding presence, animatedly directed the preparations. Beside her, Sonny, the keen-eyed tracker, scanned the surrounding woods, his senses alert for any signs of movement. Doyle, a seasoned ex-Delta Force operator with an air of quiet confidence, tended to the fire, ensuring the flames flickered brightly against the encroaching darkness.

As they cooked, a dark tension hung in the air, for beyond the flickering light of the campfire and the sheltering embrace of the Cedar Tree Hills, an insidious evil lurked in the shadows, watching and waiting for the perfect moment to strike.

CHAPTER NINE

HUNT FOR EDWARD

0300 HOURS
PRESENT-DAY
THE CEDAR TREE HILLS, EDWARD'S ISLAND

The gentle sound of rustling breaks the stillness of the night, stirring Doyle from a deep, dreamless sleep. As he lies wrapped in his sleeping bag, he slowly blinks awake, his senses sharpening. The faint light of the moon filters through the dense canopy of trees overhead, casting dappled shadows that dance across the forest floor.

He turns to his right and sees Deborah, her face illuminated by an ethereal glow, eyes wide and unblinking. "Don't move," she whispers urgently, her voice a hushed tremor that cuts through the night's quiet.

Feeling a rush of adrenaline, Doyle scans the campsite for Sonny, his heart pounding in his chest. Just as he shifts to look behind him, he hears Sonny's voice, low and tense, breaking the silence like a crack of thunder. "It's a shape-shifter up in the tree, spying on us," he warns, a note of alarm piercing his usually steady tone.

Doyle's pulse races as he processes the chilling implication of Sonny's words, his mind grappling with the unnerving reality of an unseen predator lurking in the darkness, watching their every move. The air is thick with tension, and the comforting warmth of their campfire feels suddenly fragile, surrounded by the shadows of the towering trees that loom over them.

The shape-shifter, now assuming the agile form of a small, bushy-tailed squirrel, clings to a gnarled branch high above them, its bright, inquisitive eyes scanning the ground below. With its soft, rust-colored fur glimmering in the mottled moonlight, the creature appears both adorable and cunning. Suddenly, a low, resonant growl rumbles from Sonny, echoing through the stillness of the forest. The unexpected sound startles the shape-shifter, and in an instant, it transforms into a graceful owl, its large, amber eyes wide with surprise. With powerful strokes of its wings, it ascends into the air, feathers catching the light as it glides seamlessly into the dense, shadowy canopy above, leaving only a whisper of movement in its wake.

"It's gone," Sonny said reassuringly, his voice calm and steady, a soothing balm against the night's fears as Doyle rolled onto his back. The tension in his shoulders began to ease like a balloon slowly deflating. "Shape-shifters, dwarfs, fairies, and even cave trolls! It feels like every enchanting tale my parents spun during bedtime has spilled into reality," Doyle whispered to Deborah, his eyes wide with a mixture of wonder and disbelief, reflecting the starlit sky above.

Deborah chuckled, a melodic sound, like wind chimes, cutting through the lingering unease that hung in the air like morning fog. "Where do you think the writers found the inspiration for those fantastical stories?" she teased, a playful glint sparkling in her eyes, like mischief captured in moonlight.

"I guess it's okay as long as no zombies are lurking around," Doyle replied, a hint of trepidation creeping into his voice.

Deborah sat up in her sleeping bag, the fabric rustling softly as she shifted. "Well, I hate to tell you this," she said with a coy smile, "but...I'm just teasing, darling. Zombies are not real."

Not far away, beyond the jagged expanse of grey granite boulders, Edward stands resolutely in the modest confines of his compound's office, holding a cigar in his six-fingered hand. He is a stocky figure, exuding strength, with broad shoulders that hint at a life of hard work. A shock of unruly dark hair frames his large, square head, and his skin bears the distinctive light green hue that gives him an otherworldly appearance.

Having endured a tragic accident that resulted in the amputation of both his legs below the knees, Edward stands at just over four feet tall, a stature that contrasts sharply with the imposing nature of his surroundings. His robotic feet, sleek and precision-engineered, are affixed to his knees, allowing him to move with surprising agility. With each step, he bounces side to side, a dynamic reminder of his resilience and determination to navigate the challenges of his life. The office around him carries the faint scent of machinery and the soft hum of electronics, a testament to his ingenuity and adaptability in a world that often underestimates him.

Two grotesque cave trolls towered in front of Edward, their thick, leathery skin mottled with dark patches and their sharp claws gleaming in the low light. The flickering shadows cast by the dim lanterns accentuated their hulking forms, making them even more menacing. "Deborah and her new boyfriend will soon launch an assault on our compound; we must prepare for battle," Edward announced, his voice steady yet urgent as he hopped toward the intricately carved desk, the surface cluttered with maps and strange artifacts.

"We will destroy them, master," one of the trolls growled, its gravelly voice rumbling like an approaching storm, filled with unwavering loyalty.

With a swift, practiced motion, Edward grasped a leather whip embellished with arcane symbols from the edge of the desk. The leather was cracked in places, a testament to its frequent, forceful use. As he bounced into the adjoining room, an air of dread filled the space, heavy with tension and the scent of damp earth. There, two officers from the crashed disk were held captive by Edward, their wrists bound firmly with thick, frayed ropes that cut into their skin. One officer's eyes were wide with fear, while the other clenched his jaw in defiance.

In a sudden burst of action, Edward whipped the whip through the air, letting it crack against the back of one officer with a sharp snap. The officer let out a piercing scream that echoed off the stone walls, a gut-wrenching sound that signaled his pain. "You will explain to me why your flying disk was hovering over my island!" Edward bellowed, his voice full of fury, a tempest of emotions swirling in his steely gaze as his breath came quick, fueled by rage and the thirst for answers.

Edward hopped around in front of the two officers, his eyes glinting with a twisted enthusiasm. "You have very little time left to explain your actions before Deborah arrives," he taunted, his sickly smile growing wider. "If I don't have the answers by then, your story will come to an end, and you will surely die."

One of the officers, visibly shaken but trying to maintain composure, spoke up. "We were en route to the mainland of New Zion, departing from Atlantis, when we encountered a catastrophic malfunction with our flying disk. The system failed, causing us to veer off course and unintentionally fly over your territory."

Edward's expression darkened, and he shouted, "I don't believe you for a second!" He took a menacing hop closer to them. "You were searching for my drug operations. Everyone knows there's a no-fly zone over this island, set in place by the Senate of Atlantis to protect my interests!"

As the tension thickened in the air, the officers exchanged worried glances, realizing the precariousness of their situation.

A sharp, jarring ring pierced through the intercom, startling both officers and making them jump instinctively. "Looks like the ringing phone saved you two for now," Edward quipped, an evil laugh escaping his lips as he bounced from side to side on his feet, eager to pick up the call.

As Edward grabbed the phone, he instantly recognized his father's authoritative tone, Counselor Folly. "Yes, I know she is on the island," he said, trying to keep his composure.

Folly's voice boomed through the receiver, filled with urgency and menace. "The officers, along with Deborah and Doyle, must never leave that island alive," he ordered, his words heavy with threat.

Edward's expression darkened, and a deep frown etched itself across his forehead as he absorbed the gravity of the situation. "You realize that if I kill Deborah, I'm effectively signing my own death warrant," he replied, his voice tinged with frustration, the oppressive weight of his father's demand pressing down on him like an anchor.

In the background, the officers heard Folly's loud command: "I just gave you an order!"

Edward's gaze shifted to the two imposing cave trolls who had just lumbered into the room, their hulking figures casting long shadows on the walls. "I am a drug dealer, not a hitman!" he shouted, a mixture of defiance and desperation in his tone. "You have plenty of hitmen working for you, Father!" With that, he slammed the phone back into its cradle, the sound echoing sharply in the tense atmosphere, a stark contrast to the simmering chaos surrounding him.

Edward turned to the trolls, "Get outside and make sure your men are ready for what's coming," he directed, then hopped back into his office and slammed the door.

Back at the camp, Doyle lay on his back under the vast starry sky, drifting into a peaceful slumber. Suddenly, he felt an unexpected snugness and opened his eyes to find that Deborah had slid into his sleeping bag beside him. Her warmth enveloped him, her body pressing gently against his.

"What in the world are you doing?" he exclaimed, a mix of surprise and annoyance in his voice as he scrambled to escape the confines of the sleeping bag.

"Oh, honey," she replied, a playful grin spreading across her face, her eyes glimmering like stars in the warm firelight. "I just wanted to cuddle until dawn. It's absolutely freezing out here!"

Doyle shifted his gaze towards Sonny, who was nestled comfortably by the crackling campfire, a fragrant plume of smoke curling lazily from his pipe into the crisp night air. "Thanks for the warning, bud," he muttered, a bemused smile tugging at the corners of his lips. The dazzling glow of the fire offered a stark contrast to the biting chill of the night, enveloping the scene in a blend of coziness and delightful chaos beneath the sprawling tapestry of the night sky.

"That sounds like a brilliant idea. I'm heading over to join Sonny and enjoy a cigar," Doyle declared, casting a glance at Deborah.

Deborah, nestled snugly in Doyle's thick sleeping bag, propped herself up against a cozy mound of fabric, her eyes sparkling with mischief. "You have no idea what you're missing out on, darling," she teased, a playful smile dancing on her lips.

"What I'm missing is the simple pleasure of a good cigar," Doyle replied, his voice a mix of exasperation and frustration. He fumbled through his pack and retrieved a cigar, his hands trembling slightly with anticipation and perhaps a hint of nerves. As he struck the match and lit the cigar, the warm glow flickered briefly before settling into a steady ember. "You know, you really ought to seek help with those wild desires of yours," he continued, exhaling a puff of fragrant smoke into the cool night air. "I've witnessed countless things throughout my years, but you truly take the cake with this hybrid control aura you exude. Honestly, how is a man supposed to resist you? We're not that strong," he rambled, taking another deep draw from his cigar, the rich, earthy scent wafting around them like an intoxicating cloak.

"Relax, darling. I'm just teasing; I promise I won't push you into anything you're uncomfortable with," Deborah said playfully as she climbed out of the sleeping bag, her lighthearted smile softening the cool morning air.

Doyle continued to gaze into the flickering flames of the campfire, the warmth illuminating his troubled expression. "That's a relief," he mumbled, his voice barely above a whisper.

The group remained gathered around the fire, the crackle of the embers mingling with the sounds of the waking forest as the first rays of dawn pierced the night's deep shadows. With his nerves finally settling, Doyle took a deep breath and began rolling up his sleeping bag, methodically stuffing it into his backpack as he prepared for the day's task.

Sonny, always a practical thinker, carefully extinguished the campfire remnants, ensuring that no ember remained to prevent any chance of rekindling. He used a nearby branch to stir the ashes, confirming that nothing would smolder beneath the surface.

Meanwhile, Deborah wandered over to the nearby crystal-clear stream. The soothing rush of water filled her ears, providing a serene backdrop as she leaned down to splash cool water on her face. The sensation invigorated her, sharpening her senses and preparing her for the challenging journey ahead.

Upon returning to the campsite, Deborah gathered her gear and presented her plan with determination. "We will move toward Edwards' compound and position ourselves on a high cliff that offers a clear view of it. Once we're in place, Sonny, you will deploy your small drone to fly over the compound and conduct a thorough search for the officers held captive there." Her eyes sparkled with resolve as she envisioned the operation unfolding.

"Yes, ma'am," Sonny replied, his tone firm and respectful.

Deborah pivoted to face Doyle, her brow knit with concern. "You'll need to maintain your position at the back of our group and keep a sharp lookout for any possible ambushes from cave trolls. These creatures are notoriously sly, often hiding in the shadowy recesses of caves or hollowing out small niches in the rocky terrain from which to launch their surprise attacks."

Doyle removed his 9mm handgun from its holster, the steel glinting in the sunlight as he meticulously checked the magazine, ensuring it was ready for action. "Rest easy, I'll make sure our route is clear," he said confidently, his gaze darting across the landscape.

With their roles defined, the group drew strength from the familiar sight of Cedar Tree Hills receding behind them, its towering trees and protective canopy replaced by the stark, unforgiving granite fields that lay ahead. The rocky expanse spread out like a vast, open canvas, leading them toward Edward's location. The air, charged with tension and anticipation, each footfall resonating against the hard ground as they pressed forward, aware of the potential dangers hidden in the rugged wilderness.

The sun had climbed high above the morning horizon, casting golden beams that warmed the already humid air. Doyle, feeling the oppressive heat seeping into his clothes, removed his well-worn hat and wiped the rivulets of sweat that trickled down his brow. "It's muggy already," he commented, glancing at his companions as they edged carefully along the narrow, winding path carved between two imposing boulders, their surfaces rugged and speckled with lichen.

Before Deborah could respond, a massive cave troll erupted from a dark fissure in the stone, its hulking frame a blur of motion as it smashed into Doyle, sending him sprawling backward. The troll loomed ominously over him, its beady eyes glinting with menace as it raised a jagged, rusted sword, preparing to deliver a crushing blow.

Instinctively, Deborah grasped her staff, its cool, solid wood a reassuring presence in her hands. "Stop!" she commanded, her voice cutting through the tension like a knife. The troll hesitated, momentarily taken aback by the sudden challenge. Seizing this fleeting opportunity, Deborah swung her staff with swift precision, the enchanted wood slicing through the air before it connected with the troll's thick neck. In a brutal arc, the troll's head, now severed, rolled down the cliffside and landed with a loud splash in a secluded pond below.

As the lifeless body of the troll crashed down heavily onto Doyle, pinning him to the ground with a resounding thud, the serene silence was broken only by the gentle lapping of water against the pond's edge, creating a rhythmic backdrop. Straining beneath the weight of the grotesque creature, Doyle grunted as he pushed the troll aside, the foul stench of its decay filling his nostrils as he rolled to his feet, adrenaline coursing through his veins. He glanced back at the fallen monster, its mottled skin glistening in the dappled sunlight filtering through the trees. "That thing attacked with astonishing speed," he remarked, his voice edged with disbelief and apprehension.

Turning to Deborah, Sonny's expression was serious, his brow furrowed in concern. "I can't shake the feeling that we're walking straight into a trap by continuing this way," he cautioned, his tone low and urgent.

Deborah, her hands stained with the remnants of a recent battle, meticulously wiped the blood from her staff with a ragged cloth before securing it firmly against her back. "I share your unease, Sonny. It's prudent to veer away from the trail and navigate the ridges instead," she asserted, her voice steady and commanding against the backdrop of uncertainty.

With a shared sense of purpose, the three companions climbed the rugged hills strewn with granite boulders, the rocks' sharp edges contrasting with the barren ground beneath their feet. As they hiked along the narrow ridge, a breathtaking panorama unfolded before them: the shimmering bay stretched out like a vast, sapphire canvas, and their ship lay anchored, its sails fluttering softly in the gentle morning breeze.

Upon reaching the final crest, they paused to take in the imposing sight of Edward's compound sprawled below, its fortified walls casting long shadows in the early sunlight.

Sonny knelt, carefully extracting the drone from the side of his pack, its sleek, metallic surface glinting in the light. Deborah and Doyle positioned themselves behind a large boulder, the cool stone pressing against their backs as they focused intently on Sonny's movements. The air was thick with anticipation as he calibrated the drone, preparing to send it soaring above the compound, ready to gather crucial information amid the unsettling stillness of their surroundings.

Doyle squinted through the high-powered binoculars, his pulse quickening as the drone gracefully glided above the sprawling compound, its propellers whirring softly in the still air. "I can make out several cave trolls camouflaged among the rocky outcrops along the trails we were following," he reported, a blend of relief and urgency in his voice as he scanned the rugged landscape.

"Sonny, that was an astute decision to divert us from that path," Deborah acknowledged, her eyes darting between the forest's shadowy corners and the aerial view. The tension in her voice was obvious, mixed with admiration for Sonny's sharp instincts.

Sonny, jaw set in intense concentration, focused on a compact handheld screen. The bright display cast a sharp, artificial light that emphasized the deep furrows of determination on his forehead. "Deborah, take a look at this," he urged, deftly tapping the screen to enhance the drone's live feed. On the screen, two pilots appeared, their figures dimly outlined in the murky corners of a small, poorly lit room nestled within the compound's largest, foreboding structure. Their wrists were cruelly bound above their heads with rough rope, forcing them to lean awkwardly against the stark, cold cement walls. The shadows they cast danced ominously with each flicker of the weak overhead bulb.

Deborah stood with composed authority, the intricate design of her staff glinting as she unlatched it from her back. "Here's the plan," she explained, her voice calm yet firm, cutting through the tension in the air. "You two will remain here until I breach the compound. Once I neutralize the cave trolls, come back to the trail and enter through the main gate."

"How exactly are you going to pull this off?" Doyle asked, his eyes wide with a mix of admiration and concern. Just then, with an explosive surge of power, Deborah leaped high into the air, her body soaring against the morning sky, a silhouette against the blue sky. She floated gracefully down, landing with precision just inside the formidable walls of the compound.

"Holy shit. Did you see that?" Doyle exclaimed, his voice a blend of disbelief and awe as he turned to Sonny, the air buzzing with adrenaline.

Sonny glanced at Doyle with a confident smile. "She is one of the strongest hybrids in our realm, unmatched in her abilities. Watch closely; she alone will vanquish the cave trolls."

As the dust settled from Deborah's dynamic entrance into the compound, three massive cave trolls, their grotesque features contorted in fury, charged toward her. Undeterred, Deborah confidently spun her intricately carved staff, the polished wood glinting in the sunlight, as she sprinted toward the advancing trolls. With a sudden deftness, she dropped to one knee, the ground trembling beneath her, and swung her staff with precision. In a swift motion, she severed the towering trolls' legs, their guttural roars echoing through the air.

Doyle and Sonny stood transfixed, their eyes wide with a mix of awe and horror as they heard the trolls' anguished screams. With a measured and deliberate demeanor, Deborah approached the fallen beasts. As she neared them, she methodically beheaded each troll, her swift movements a testament to her formidable skill and strength. The scene was both grim and awe-inspiring, showcasing her power in the face of danger.

"Look, Doyle," Sonny exclaimed, gesturing toward the last of the cave trolls as they scrambled away in sheer terror. "They really are a cowardly bunch, aren't they?"

Deborah raised her gaze to the rugged outline of the ridge above them, her eyes narrowing in determination. She signaled for Doyle and Sonny to move quickly toward the compound's entrance, her urgency clear. Once satisfied that they were on their way, she turned her attention back to the compound's shadowy depths. "Edward!" she called out, her voice echoing slightly in the stillness, hoping to reach him within the stone walls.

Sonny entered the gate first, holding his hand up to catch his small drone. After clipping it back onto his pack, he raced to Deborah's side. Doyle entered with a slower pace, watching for a surprise attack. "I think all the cave trolls have abandoned their positions," he said, walking to join Deborah and Sonny.

As one of the heavy doors of the compound creaked open, Edward emerged, hopping from side to side in an exaggerated manner. His expression was one of irritation mixed with bemusement. "Hello, Deborah. I see you've taken it upon yourself to eliminate several of my men."

Deborah met his gaze steadily. "Those aren't men; they're soulless trolls, and I simply put them out of their misery," she responded, her tone icy and unapologetic.

Doyle, observing the scene, couldn't help but chuckle at Edward's unexpected height, or rather, lack of it. He raised an eyebrow and asked, "What's with those ridiculously long arms?" His laughter bubbled up, filling the space with a mix of confusion and amusement.

With a tone dripping with sarcasm, Deborah replied, "He had an unfortunate accident that resulted in the loss of his legs from the knee down."

Edward shot a glare at Doyle, his eyes narrowing. "Is this your new boyfriend?" he questioned, his voice laced with disdain. Then, turning back to Deborah, he added sharply, "And just to set the record straight, I didn't have an accident; you were the one who severed my legs with that staff."

"You cut his legs off? Damn!" Doyle exclaimed, laughter spilling from his lips like a bubbling brook. The humor danced in his eyes, a stark contrast to the tension in the air.

"You might find it amusing now," Edward retorted, his voice rising with indignation, "but I assure you, I'll be the one laughing in the end." His words hung in the air, heavy and defiant.

With a smug grin, Doyle leaned back, crossing his arms. "Really? You're just an ankle-biter, barely taller than a dwarf. Hardly intimidating!" His mockery echoed like a taunt.

In response, Edward pressed a sleek button on his watch, and a loud, mechanical roar erupted from behind the building. Suddenly, a driverless golf cart surged into view, tires screeching against the pavement as it raced toward him. Without hesitation, Edward leaped onto the back seat, gripping the edges as the cart zoomed away with a burst of speed.

"He's trying to escape!" Sonny shouted, panic rising in his voice as he pointed at the speeding vehicle that was rapidly disappearing down the winding road, its tires screeching against the pavement.

"Sonny! You need to follow him while Doyle and I work on freeing the hostages!" Deborah commanded, her tone firm and resolute.

"On it!" Sonny replied, determination fueling his pace as he broke into a sprint after Edward's vehicle. Meanwhile, Deborah and Doyle rushed into the dimly lit building, their hearts pounding as they navigated through the corridor to the back room where the two pilots were held captive.

"Quickly, remove their gags," Deborah instructed, her hands steady as she expertly cut through the ropes binding the officers' wrists. "They'll need to join us as we pursue Edward," she explained, glancing anxiously at the door, wondering how much time they had before their adversary vanished completely.

Sonny sprinted down the road, determination propelling him forward as he chased after Edward. With a steady hand, he drew one of his pistols from its holster, feeling the cool metal against his palm. He focused his aim on the golf cart that Edward was hastily maneuvering and pulled the trigger. A brilliant laser beam zipped from the barrel, striking the golf cart and sending it careening off course, ultimately crashing into a cluster of trees.

"Deborah, I've successfully disabled his cart. Edward is now limping into the forest," Sonny reported, his breath coming in quick gasps.

"Excellent work, Sonny," Deborah said with a nod of approval. "Take your time tracking him. We'll be ready to move as soon as we get the officers cleaned up."

Edward, sitting behind a tree, retrieved his phone from his pocket. "I need extraction immediately!" he yelled into it. "I'm not dying here today."

CHAPTER TEN

THE CHASE

1100 HOURS
PRESENT-DAY
EDWARD'S COMPOUND

Sonny approached the wrecked golf cart, its twisted frame partially hidden by overgrown bushes, when he spotted Edward slip into a narrow cave opening nestled off a dirt trail to the east. With a sense of urgency, Sonny retrieved a compact drone from his backpack, its sleek design reflecting sunlight as he gently tossed it into the air. He quickly accessed a small handheld device and carefully entered the drone's mission parameters. Once programmed, the drone buzzed to life, ascending gracefully before hovering steadily above the cave entrance, its camera lens focused on the shadowy depths beyond.

Deborah stepped out of the compound, her boots crunching on the gravel path, followed closely by the two Atlantis officers and Doyle. They quickened their pace, jogging down the narrow road to rendezvous with Sonny. "Did you see where Edward went?" she asked, her voice steady despite the urgency of their mission.

"Yes, he entered that small cave over there, where my drone is currently hovering," Sonny replied, pointing toward a nondescript entrance partly obscured by overgrown foliage.

Deborah squinted at the cave's dark opening, her brow furrowing with concern. "If Edward has ventured into the tunnel system of the cave trolls, we could be facing quite a delay in flushing him out. Those tunnels are extensive and treacherous."

Sonny locked eyes with Deborah, a hint of worry etched on his face. "Should we leave him behind and head to the ship?"

"No. We can't let Edward escape. Send your drone in to scout the cave. We need to know his exact location and the layout of those tunnels before making any decisions," Deborah instructed firmly, her mind racing with strategy and the implications of their next steps.

The drone descended gracefully, hovering just in front of the cave entrance before releasing two smoke bombs that detonated with a faint hiss, filling the dark opening with thick, swirling clouds of smoke. As the smoke billowed outward, the drone boldly ventured inside, its infrared radar scanning the interior for heat signatures. "Deborah, I can confirm the cave is just a small room and not connected to the tunnel system; Edward is alone in there," Sonny asserted, his eyes glued to the vivid screen of his handheld device, the data flickering before him in real time.

Moments later, the drone emerged from the cave, trailing behind Edward, who stumbled into view, coughing and gagging as the acrid smoke filled his lungs. Disoriented yet determined, he continued east along a narrow dirt trail that wound through the dense underbrush. Sonny quickly summoned the drone back to his side, his attention suddenly drawn to a second movement as something else burst from the cave. "Two Jinn are rushing out of the cave, and they're following Edward!" Sonny yelled, his voice rising with urgency.

"What are Jinn?" Doyle asked, his curiosity piqued as he watched Deborah, determined and focused, make her way down the dirt trail in hot pursuit of Edward.

"They are supernatural beings known for their extraordinary powers. One of them was likely the shapeshifter that visited our campsite last night," Deborah explained succinctly, her mind racing as she quickened her pace to catch up with Edward.

Doyle turned his gaze towards the two officers, an incredulous expression crossing his face. "Those are Jinn, whatever in the world that means!" he exclaimed, rolling his eyes in frustration.

Deborah came to a sudden halt, her eyes narrowing with fierce determination as she assessed the situation. "Doyle, I need you to stay here with the two officers. They do not have the strength to keep up with us," she instructed, her voice unwavering and authoritative. "We'll return as soon as we've apprehended Edward."

"Understood," Doyle replied, his voice calm and steady despite the chaotic environment surrounding them. The air was thick with tension, and the distant sounds of commotion echoed through the area. "Alright, everyone, take a seat in the golf cart. I'll stand guard and keep a lookout," he said, his gaze fixed on the path ahead, ensuring that he would monitor their surroundings as Deborah and Sonny disappeared into the shadows, their figures growing smaller as they ventured deeper into the unknown.

As Edward trudged along the narrow path, he came upon a small, glistening stream, its crystal-clear waters bubbling over smooth stones. He scanned the area, frustration gnawing at him; there was no feasible place to cross, and his short, damaged legs were far too inept to leap over the shimmering expanse.

"Edward! You might as well give yourself up!" Deborah's voice echoed through the trees, strong and commanding, slicing through the forest's serenity.

"Never!" Edward retorted defiantly, adrenaline surging through him. He turned to face the two Jinn, their forms shifting like shadows, exuding an air of menace. "Kill her."

With a sudden burst of energy, the Jinn launched themselves into the air, their bodies graceful and fluid as they ascended into the gnarled branches of a majestic tree that towered above the dirt trail. They perched on a thick limb, their eyes glinting with anticipation, ready to spring down as Deborah approached, a wicked smile on their faces.

Just as they prepared to unleash their attack, a radiant, shimmering net cascaded from above, ensnaring the Jinn in a dazzling web of magic. The intricate patterns of the net sparkled in the sunlight, and despite their thrashing and screeching, the Jinn found themselves hopelessly trapped, unable to break free from the enchantment.

"It's a magic net that you can't cut," Deborah proclaimed, standing resolutely off to the side of the trail, her staff crackling with energy as it pointed menacingly at the ensnared creatures. The serene sound of the stream gurgled softly behind her, a stark contrast to the rising tension in the air, as the forest held its breath in anticipation of what would come next.

After witnessing Deborah successfully trap the Jinn, Edward sprang toward the nearest boulder that jutted out of the stream. However, his feet slipped on the slick surface, and he tumbled into the cool, rushing water below.

"Get up, little man," Sonny said, a smirk playing on his lips as he reached into the water to pull Edward out, dragging him onto the muddy bank.

As Edward sprawled on his belly, gasping for breath, panic washed over him. "Don't hurt me!" he pleaded, his voice trembling with fear.

With a sharp, forceful kick, Sonny flipped Edward onto his back, standing over him like a dark shadow, his figure exuding an unmistakable air of menace. "I ought to behead you right here," he sneered, his eyes alight with a dangerous blend of amusement and seething rage, reflecting the brutality of their confrontation.

Deborah approached with deliberate steps, her expression cold as she looked down at Edward, who was struggling to catch his breath. He squinted against the harsh glare of the sunlight, a sly smile creeping onto his face despite the situation. "Hey, babe. How have you been?" he asked, trying to maintain an air of charm.

Without hesitation, Deborah brought her staff down sharply against his chest, the impact resounding through the air. "Don't 'hey, babe' me!" she retorted, her voice firm and unwavering.

Edward rolled onto his side, a cry of pain escaping his lips. "You crazy witch!" he yelled, the mix of disbelief and frustration clear in his tone as he clutched his chest.

Doyle stood beside the golf cart and glanced at the two officers. "You guys okay?" he asked, his voice tinged with concern. Both officers nodded reassuringly, but Doyle suddenly heard an unusual rustling to his left. He turned and squinted, confused by the sight of a tiny bearded man perched on a branch in a nearby tree.

"Who are you?" Doyle asked.

"I am Ogden. I live on this island," the little man announced, his high-pitched voice punctuated by the gentle puffing of his intricately carved pipe, the smoke curling elegantly into the air.

Doyle flashed a smile at the officers before directing his attention back to Ogden. "Are you a Jinn?" he inquired, curiosity sparking in his eyes.

Ogden let out a hearty laugh, the sound playful and warm. "No, no. I am a wizard fairy," he corrected, his eyes twinkling with mischief.

Doyle leaned in closer, eyebrows raised with curiosity. "Oh, a wizard, huh? What can I do for you today?" His voice was laced with intrigue, clearly eager to learn more about this unexpected encounter.

Ogden, the wizard, exhaled a puff of smoke from his pipe, a calm smile playing at the corners of his lips. "I don't require anything from you," he replied, his tone measured and serene. "I am simply here, observing the world while I enjoy my morning smoke."

Doyle nodded thoughtfully, tapping his finger as he considered the moment. "I see. In that case, I think I'll join you for a smoke," he said, pulling a cigar from his pocket and preparing to light it.

With a glimmer of amusement in his eyes, Ogden continued, "Deborah asked me to keep an eye on you."

Doyle raised an eyebrow, puffing on his cigar as he replied, "Oh, really? I didn't hear her ask you to do that."

Ogden set his pipe aside and looked Doyle in the eye, his expression becoming more serious. "She spoke not to me in words," he explained. "Her thoughts reached out to me directly, urging me to ensure your well-being."

"Her thoughts? How does that work exactly?" Doyle inquired, his brow furrowing in curiosity. Ogden, deep in contemplation, slowly closed his eyes as he sensed Doyle's gaze upon him. "What?" Doyle asked, turning around with a puzzled expression. "I heard someone say 'over here,'" he responded, scanning the area and looking at the two officers nearby. "Did one of you say something?"

With a knowing smile, Ogden opened his eyes and replied, "That is how it works," as he leisurely puffed on his pipe, the smoke swirling around him. The atmosphere was thick with intrigue, and the officers exchanged glances, caught between amusement and confusion at the cryptic exchange.

Sonny meticulously finished securing Edward to a sturdy log, the rough ropes digging into the wood as he tightened them. "Should I go find Doyle to help carry Edward back to the ship?" he inquired, glancing at the horizon.

"No," Deborah replied, her voice firm, just as four dwarves emerged from the dense foliage of the forest. Their stout forms were visible as they stepped into the clearing, each one clad in colorful clothing and carrying an air of confidence. "These gentlemen will assist us in transporting him."

"That should work well enough," Sonny agreed, relieved by the unexpected assistance.

The dwarves approached Edward with an air of determination, effortlessly lifting him from the ground and hoisting him over their shoulders. They began to follow Deborah up the narrow dirt trail that wound through the trees. As they moved, Edward struggled against his bonds, raising his voice in protest. "Deborah, my father is not going to approve of this! What you're doing is outright kidnapping!" he yelled, his voice echoing off the trees.

"Kidnapping? I think not," Deborah retorted, her tone cutting through the forest air. "You broke multiple laws of Atlantis when you shot down the flying disk and killed two innocent pilots. And let's not forget the way you tortured the two officers you captured!" She shot back, her eyes narrowing as they marched onward, unwavering in their mission.

As they cautiously navigated the tangled underbrush beneath the sprawling limb that ensnared the Jinn in Deborah's intricate netting, she tilted her head upwards, her sharp green eyes locking onto theirs.

"If I free you from this trap, will you return to your own affairs, or will you choose to shadow our steps?"

The two Jinn exchanged furtive glances, their skin shimmering like rippling water in dusk's glow. One of them, his voice resonating like distant thunder, replied, "We shall surely resume our own business and not interfere."

"You cowards!" Edward shouted, his voice an angry crack in the forest's hush, as he dangled precariously from the stout log above, his frustration showing.

With a swift, practiced motion, Deborah brought her staff down sharply upon Edward's shoulder, knocking him into unconsciousness with a soft thud. She then turned her attention back to the Jinn, her expression fierce and unwavering. "Very well," she pronounced, the air crackling with her resolve, "I will grant you your freedom." Her gaze bore into them, a warning etched in her tone. "But be forewarned: if you choose to follow us, I will unleash all my wrath upon you, and nothing will shield you from it."

"No ma'am," the Jinn replied, their voices steady and low, as they inclined their heads in a gesture of respect. "We shall not intrude upon your journey." The tension in the air lifted slightly, yet an undercurrent of distrust lingered between them, like an unseen storm ready to break.

Deborah raised her staff, a beautifully carved piece of wood imbued with magical symbols, and pointed it at the shimmering net that ensnared the Jinn. With a crackle of energy and a shower of sparks, the net disintegrated, freeing the ethereal beings. The Jinn, glowing with delight, ascended gracefully into the lush green branches of a towering tree, their laughter echoing like chimes in the wind.

As the group resumed their trek along the winding trail, they soon caught sight of Doyle, who stood beside the two officers, their expressions brightening at the party's approach. "Good afternoon!" Doyle exclaimed, waving enthusiastically.

"Sonny, please gather some dry wood and start a fire," Deborah directed, her tone firm yet warm. "We need to have a hearty lunch before we embark on our journey back to the ship." The scent of fresh pine and earth surrounded them, promising the comfort of a meal amidst the tension.

The dwarfs expertly suspended the log with Edward secured between two sturdy trees, creating a makeshift anchor as Sonny knelt beside a pile of twigs and kindling to ignite the fire. "Ma'am, we will go catch some fish for our meal," one of the dwarfs announced to Deborah, his voice filled with determination and purpose.

"Thank you," Deborah replied warmly, her eyes reflecting gratitude for their kindness.

Doyle stepped closer to Deborah, his demeanor serious yet friendly. "We have a guest," he said, gesturing toward Ogden, who remained perched in the branches of the tree, observing the scene with curious interest. The gentle rustling of leaves accompanied their conversation, adding a sense of tranquility to the moment.

Deborah turned her gaze toward Ogden, her eyes shimmering with gratitude. "Thank you," she said, her voice soft but full of warmth. Ogden returned her gaze with a gentle smile, his eyes filled with kindness. "You are most welcome, Deborah," he replied, his voice echoing with sincerity. As the last words hung in the air, a mystical glow enveloped him, and he gradually faded away, leaving behind a faint shimmer that lingered in the space where he once sat.

The dwarves returned, proudly hauling two strings of fresh fish, glistening in the sunlight. "That was impressively quick," Doyle remarked, his eyes gleaming with satisfaction.

"Sonny, we need to move swiftly to prepare lunch," Deborah said, her tone urgent. She scanned the surrounding area for any signs of impending danger. "Even though we managed to scare off the cave trolls for now, they are likely to return with greater numbers."

"Yes, ma'am," Sonny replied, acknowledging the seriousness of her words.

The dwarves busily set to work, chopping and mixing ingredients to create a delicious feast for the group. One of them ventured into the nearby woods, gathering vibrant mushrooms and fragrant herbs to enhance the meal's flavors. The air filled with the tantalizing aroma of their cooking, promising a satisfying reprieve from their recent troubles.

The group sat around the crackling fire, savoring their simple but satisfying lunch. Sunlight filtered through the trees, casting playful shadows on the ground. "Alright, Sonny, please extinguish the fire carefully to prevent any forest mishaps," Deborah commanded, her voice steady and authoritative. "Doyle, you'll be responsible for assisting the officers as we make our way back to the ship."

Turning her attention to the dwarves, she added, "Thank you all for the delicious lunch. We truly appreciate your hospitality. Now, we need your strength to carry Edward down to the bay."

"Yes, ma'am. We're on it," one of the dwarfs replied with a nod, showing determination to help their friends. The others gathered around, ready to lend their support as they prepared for the next leg of the journey.

"We're only about an hour's hike from the bay, and the trail is nearly flat the entire way," Deborah explained to the group, her voice steady and reassuring as she surveyed the surroundings.

Doyle carefully helped the two officers to their feet, ensuring they were steady, then fell back to walk just behind them. The four dwarves, straining slightly under the weight of Edward, trudged along behind Sonny, who confidently led the way with a determined stride. Deborah trailed closely behind the dwarves, her senses heightened as she scanned the dense forest around them, alert for any signs of lurking cave trolls that might threaten their journey. The dappled sunlight filtering through the treetops provided a sense of calm, but she remained vigilant, ready to react at the first hint of danger.

Doyle pressed the small, metallic button on his sleek earpiece, and a burst of static crackled through the device, filling the humid air with a faint buzz. "Come in, Eddie," he said, his voice steady and authoritative, betraying none of the urgency that quickened his pulse.

"Go ahead, Doyle," Eddie's voice flowed back, calm and composed. He was stationed high above their modest boat, cleverly camouflaged among the dense, vibrant green foliage of a towering palm tree. From his lofty perch, he surveyed the lively surroundings, a canopy of leaves rustling in the gentle breeze, and the shimmering ocean stretching out before them, glistening with an array of blues under the bright tropical sun.

"We're currently en route to the bay," Doyle continued, his tone unwavering. "Please notify The Driver to prepare a second boat for transporting Edward to the ship."

"I'm on it, Doyle," Eddie responded promptly, his voice unwavering as the sound of his miniature propellers whirred to life. With deft precision, he took off, soaring through the lush treetops and leaving a light trail of disturbed leaves in his wake as he made his way to relay the crucial message.

As the group drew closer to the beach, they could smell the salty tang of the ocean mixed with the rich, earthy scents of the island's flora. They caught sight of a sleek, streamlined second boat cutting through the turquoise waters, its glistening hull reflecting the sunlight like polished silver, powered by two AI deckhands who moved with the fluid efficiency of finely tuned machines.

Eddie descended gracefully toward Doyle, "It's good to see you, sir," he called out, a note of relief softening his otherwise professional demeanor.

"Thanks, Eddie. It's good to see you, too," Doyle replied.

Meanwhile, the four dwarves, their sturdy frames and muscular arms apparent as they carefully lifted Edward, navigated him to the water's edge. The sound of their feet crunching against the coarse sand echoed softly as they laid him down with a practiced gentleness, taking care to ensure he was comfortable. With a swift, coordinated effort, they untied him, the ropes falling away like discarded burdens.

Deborah approached Edward, staff in hand, her expression a mixture of authority and annoyance. "Move, and I'll knock you again," she warned, her tone sharp and unwavering, a reminder of the tension that hung thick in the air like humidity before a storm. The surroundings suddenly felt charged, as if the very atmosphere waited for Edward's response.

"Can someone help me stand up?" Edward cried out, his voice strained with urgency as he struggled futilely to rise on his kneeless legs, which left him vulnerable and unsteady on the coarse, sun-warmed sand. Two dwarves, their faces etched with determination, quickly moved to his side, their strong hands gripping him firmly as they aided his rise. They deftly stood him up just shy of the gentle caress of the waves lapping at the shore.

Standing resolutely nearby, Deborah clutched her intricately carved staff, its polished surface gleaming in the sunlight. She positioned it against the back of Edward's head, exerting a subtle yet unmistakable authority. The atmosphere crackled with tension as two AI deckhands stepped out of their sleek, metallic boat, their movements mechanical yet precise. "We'll take control of him now, ma'am," one of the deckhands announced, his voice devoid of emotion yet commanding in its clarity.

The second deckhand raised a Taser, its electrodes glinting menacingly, and pressed it against Edward's side, asserting dominance as they led him toward the boat. With a cooperative effort, two of the dwarves lifted Edward, their muscles straining slightly as they placed him into the boat, the vessel rocking gently beneath the weight of his predicament. Once settled, the deckhands swiftly joined him, climbing aboard with an air of efficiency. As the boat's motors hummed to life, it glided away from the shore, carrying its reluctant prisoner toward the looming silhouette of the larger ship waiting in the distance, a harbinger of the uncertainty that lay ahead.

Deborah turned to the four dwarves, her expression warm with gratitude. "Thank you for your assistance," she said, extending her hand, which held four shimmering gold coins, one for each of them.

The dwarves nodded appreciatively, their eyes gleaming as they accepted the gold. "Thank you, my lady," they replied in unison, their voices a harmonious blend of respect and camaraderie, and pocketed the coins before turning to walk away.

Deborah's gaze shifted to Doyle, who stood nearby with a look of determination. "Could you please drag our boat back to the water? We need to return to our ship," she instructed, her tone both commanding and polite.

"Absolutely," Doyle replied with a confident nod. He and Sonny then grasped the sturdy ropes attached to the boat and began hauling it across the warm, sandy beach, their muscles straining slightly as they worked together to maneuver the vessel toward the gentle waves lapping at the shore.

Once the boat was afloat in the deeper waters of the bay, Sonny and Doyle carefully assisted the two officers aboard. "Doyle, please seat them in the front row," Deborah instructed, her voice steady over the gentle lapping of the waves. "You'll take your place in the back row again." This arrangement would ensure the officers had a clear view as they set out, while Doyle's position at the back would maintain the necessary balance.

Sonny grasped the oars firmly as he began to row the small boat toward the looming silhouette of the ship, its sails billowing majestically in the wind. Deborah sat comfortably next to Doyle, the ocean spray glistening on her skin.

"So, tell me, Doyle," Deborah started, her voice cutting through the sound of the waves. "How do you think we did on this mission?"

Doyle, his brow furrowed in thought, shook his head slowly. "We are far from being finished. The real challenges lie ahead. We still have to make our way back to Atlantis, and we may very well have to confront another Kraken." His expression was a mix of resolve and concern as he stared out at the horizon, contemplating the dangers that awaited them.

"Oh, we will certainly have to confront another Kraken," Deborah said, a gleam of excitement in her eyes. "Once we navigate beyond the shallows and into the open sea, I have no doubt they will be lying in wait for us, ready to strike." A confident smile played on her lips, revealing her adventurous spirit and her readiness for the challenge ahead.

Eddie the drone flew beside Doyle near the back of the boat as they made their way to the ship so that they could sail back to Atlantis.

CHAPTER ELEVEN

SAIL TO ATLANTIS

1930 HOURS
PRESENT-DAY
EDWARD'S ISLAND BAY

The enormous ship, its majestic sails billowing like great wings, gracefully turned away from the serene bay, its prow cutting through the rolling waves as it headed away from the shores of Edward's Island. With a steady resolve, it set its course back to the fabled shores of Atlantis. "We must rely on the sails to navigate these shallow waters until I can be certain we are far beyond the reach of any lurking Kraken," The Driver explained to Deborah, his sharp gaze meticulously scanning the churning sea for any ominous signs of danger. The wind howled around them, filled with the bracing aroma of salt and the exhilarating spray of the ocean. At the same time, the relentless rhythm of the waves fueled his steadfast determination to ensure their safety as they journeyed into the uncertain depths of the vast, open sea.

Deborah leaned against the ship's railing, her gaze fixed on the horizon where the sky met the sea. Turning to The Driver, she said,

"I understand the risks. Make sure the countermeasures are ready this time; we can't afford to be caught off guard by a surprise Kraken attack."

"The AI navigators have already armed the defenses," The Driver replied, his tone steady and confident as he scanned the water for any signs of movement.

"Good job", Deborah nodded thoughtfully and then asked The Driver, "Has Edward been placed in a cell yet?"

"The AI crew members have thoroughly searched him for any concealed weapons and have successfully moved him to one of the secure holding cells in the lower sections of the ship," The Driver explained, his tone efficient and factual.

Nearby, Doyle and Sonny exchanged glances as they listened to the conversation. Doyle broke the silence, saying, "Deborah, if it's all right with you, Sonny and I are going to our cabins to take showers and change into dry clothes."

Deborah offered them a warm smile. "Of course, dear. That sounds perfectly fine. I'll see you both in one hour in the captain's dining room for supper." After they nodded in agreement, she turned her attention back to The Driver. "I assume you have the chefs diligently working on our meal?"

"Yes, ma'am. They are on it and preparing a feast fit for the occasion," The Driver assured her, his tone reflecting the seriousness of his responsibilities.

As Doyle strolled away, the early evening sunlight cast a warm glow on his path. Deborah's voice echoed after him, laced with playful urgency, "Don't forget, it's a jacket and tie dinner event, darling!"

Doyle turned slightly, a smile spreading across his face as he waved, responding with a light-hearted, "Yes, ma'am." He then carefully descended the steps, his boots clicking against the surface, while Eddie, the drone, hovered faithfully behind him, its sensors whirring softly.

"Sir," Eddie interjected, his mechanical voice steady and precise, a metallic timbre that resonated in the hallway's warm light. "It seems she has quite an eye for you."

Doyle paused, a flicker of amusement crossing his face as he turned to regard the drone, its polished exterior reflecting the soft glow of the lanterns. A mischievous grin tugged at the corners of his mouth. "Tell me about it," he replied, the playful tone in his voice hinting at a sense of camaraderie. "I'm just glad others can see it too."

"It's quite obvious," Eddie responded as they crossed the threshold into their cabin.

Half an hour later, a sharp jolt reverberated through the ship, shaking the very bulkheads and sending a wave of alarm rippling through Deborah's mind. "That has to be a Kraken," she murmured to herself, a shiver running down her spine as she steeled her resolve. Without hesitation, she darted out of her suite, her heart pounding as she made her way to the bridge. As she entered, the air was thick with tension, and the sound of countermeasures hitting the water echoed ominously in the confined space.

"We have two Krakens pursuing us, one on each side!" The Driver exclaimed, his voice a mixture of urgency and authority, eyes scanning the chaos unfolding outside the ship's fortified window.

"Captain, a third Kraken is approaching from the rear!" a crew member shouted, panic evident in his wide eyes as he clutched the edge of the console, desperately trying to maintain his composure.

"Keep releasing the countermeasures!" The Driver commanded, his voice firm and unwavering as he clutched the radio tightly in his hand, urgency etched deeply across his face. The weight of the situation pressed down on him like a stormy sky. "I need the snipers positioned on the main mast, and I need them there immediately!" He turned sharply to Deborah, with intensity in his gaze. "It feels like Edward has summoned the Krakens from the abyss to attack us."

Adrenaline coursing through her veins, Deborah met The Driver's fervent gaze, her expression one of unwavering focus and determination. "That sounds exactly like something he would do," she replied, her voice steady despite the rising tension around them. "I'm grabbing my staff and heading to the deck." Each word was laced with resolve as she prepared herself to confront the looming peril that threatened to rise from the depths of the ocean waves.

"Don't get too close to the railing!" The Driver shouted over the roar of the waves, his voice laced with urgency. "I don't want anyone taking an unexpected dip in the water!"

Deborah spun around, fire flashing in her eyes. "I've been in the water with Kraken before!" she retorted, defiance ringing in her voice.

After quickly retrieving her staff from its resting place, she sprinted across the swaying deck, her heart racing with determination.

From her vantage point on the ship's deck, she spotted the two snipers expertly climbing the towering main mast, their figures sharp against the expansive sky. "Don't shoot them!" she shouted, her voice laced with urgency that cut through the salty air.

Taking their positions in the crow's nest, the two snipers steadied their rifles, their eyes narrowed as they tracked the sleek form of the Kraken gliding just below the surface, darting alongside the ship like a shadow. Deborah, her heart racing, slammed her staff powerfully against the metal deck. A resounding crack reverberated across the water, and a brilliant blue light radiated from the ship, casting shimmering reflections on the waves.

As the Krakens emerged from the shadowy depths of the ocean, their enormous, luminescent eyes reflected an ethereal glow, revealing a profound intelligence that sent a shiver racing down Deborah's spine. The water around them shimmered with an otherworldly light, heightening her sense of urgency.

With her heart pounding, Deborah shouted to The Driver, "Lower the sails and start the engine! I can't hold them off for long!" Her voice trembled with both fear and determination, resonating over the crashing waves.

The Driver, glancing back at the sprawling sea behind them, turned to the AI pilots stationed at the helm. "Lower the sails and activate the reactor. We need to reach full speed ahead, now!" His voice was steady, but urgency tinged his command as they navigated perilously close to the creatures.

Two of the three Krakens shifted their course away from the ship in a synchronized display of powerful grace, their massive bodies slicing through the water with uncanny ease. However, the last one lingered, its unblinking gaze locked onto Deborah. The air felt heavy with tension as she realized the creature was neither threatening nor retreating.

"Go on! Get out of here!" she urged, her voice rising above the sound of the roaring ocean as she watched the final Kraken slowly sink back into the depths, its massive form disappearing beneath the waves like a shadow fading into the night.

Deborah lowered her staff, watching as the shimmering blue shield of light gradually dissipated into the air like mist in the morning sun. "We're in the clear now," she remarked, her voice steady and confident as she walked past The Driver, the scent of polished metal and saltwater filling the atmosphere around them. With a purposeful stride, she made her way toward her suite, casting a glance back at him. "I'll meet you and the group in the captain's dining room shortly," she added, her eyes sparkling with determination as she disappeared down the elegant corridor.

Doyle made a grand entrance into the captain's dining room, the warm glow of softly lit chandeliers highlighting his brown sports coat, which hugged his frame just right, and his stylish fedora, tilted slightly to one side. "Where is the feast?" he inquired, his smile beaming with enthusiasm, as Deborah glided in gracefully behind him. "Oh my, you look absolutely stunning tonight," he said, his gaze sweeping over her exquisite ballroom dress. It cascaded to the floor in elegant waves, the fabric shimmering subtly with each movement, catching the light and accentuating her every curve.

The rich scents of gourmet dishes wafted through the air as The Driver approached, a welcoming smile on his face. "This way," he instructed, leading the pair toward the head of the table. The table itself was a masterpiece, meticulously set with fine china, polished silverware, and flickering candles that cast a warm, inviting glow across the room.

Sonny was already indulging in his meal, his focus solely on the delicious spread before him, as Doyle settled into the chair beside him, the enticing aroma of freshly cooked dishes enveloping him.

With a sparkling glass in hand, Deborah stood with an air of elegance, her voice ringing clear and confident. "Here's to the safe return of our brave officers and this remarkable crew," she declared, her eyes sparkling with sincerity.

"Cheers!" the group exclaimed in unison, their clinking glasses echoing joyfully against the backdrop of laughter and the evening's bustle, filling the room with warmth and shared celebration.

Just as Doyle relished the robust flavors of his first bite, Deborah looked up from her plate, her gaze piercing through the candlelit ambiance of the room. "I can sense that something is bothering you," she said, her voice laced with genuine concern.

Doyle paused, carefully savoring the texture of the food before swallowing. He lifted his napkin to wipe his mouth, a habitual gesture that gave him a moment to collect his thoughts. "Yeah, I've been mulling over this bounty hunter gig," he replied, his brow slightly furrowed.

Deborah leaned in, intrigued. "What are your thoughts on it?" she asked, her expressive eyes encouraging him to share.

Taking a slow sip of the deep crimson wine that gleamed in his glass, Doyle let its velvety richness wash over him. "I've come to the realization that this path is not for me," he confessed, the weight of his words hanging in the air between them. "After years spent in the chaos of combat, facing life-and-death situations, I find myself craving a different kind of life. Approaching sixty, I want to immerse myself in the tranquility of shared moments with Susan, savoring the quiet joys that make life worthwhile."

Deborah took a moment to digest Doyle's words, the weight of their conversation hanging in the air before she responded. "I truly understand how you feel, Doyle. However, you are not obligated to remain in your current position. There is a possibility for you to lead a quiet, unobtrusive life within the secure borders of Atlantis, away from the chaos that surrounds you."

"I've been contemplating a return to the serene mountains of North Carolina," Doyle replied, his voice tinged with nostalgia.

Deborah's expression softened into a sympathetic smile. "While I appreciate your longing for home, I'm afraid that path may be closed to you. Jonah will undoubtedly oppose your return, especially given the fact that you are considered a marked man in these troubling times."

Doyle glanced at her, confusion etched on his face. "Marked? What do you mean by that?"

Deborah's gaze grew serious. "The Shadow government has placed a target on your back due to your alleged involvement in the Senator's assassination. Moreover, there's a more pressing concern: Susan's health. If you choose to go back to the States, I fear her illness will resurface with an even darker intensity. Her cancer will not show mercy."

"Jonah boldly proclaimed that Susan has triumphed over her cancer," Doyle snapped, frustration etched on his face. Deborah shook her head slowly, her expression somber. "Only if she stays in Atlantis, where the air is pure, and the waters are healing. The harsh pollution of the outside world will ravage her immune system, and her disease will inevitably return."

"If you would excuse me," Doyle said politely to the group gathered around the table, as he rose and made his way out of the Captain's dining room. The rich scent of polished wood and the lingering aroma of a gourmet meal filled the air behind him. Stepping onto the expansive deck, he settled into one of the sturdy chairs, the ocean breeze ruffling his collar. As he lit a cigar with a practiced flick of his lighter, he noticed Deborah sauntering toward him, her expression curious.

"What's up, darling?" she inquired, her voice inviting and warm.

Doyle took a long, satisfying draw from the cigar, savoring the rich flavor before exhaling a plume of smoke. "I miss my dog, Gunner, and the majestic mountains of home," he confessed, a hint of nostalgia creeping into his tone. "But I know we can never return to that life."

Deborah's smile was bright and understanding. "I can arrange for Jonah to bring Gunner here. I've told you before that anything you desire in this world, I can make happen," she assured him, her eyes sparkling with determination.

"I'm certain Jonah would bring Gunner here if I asked him," Doyle replied, a playful grin forming on his lips. "But I get the feeling Jonah doesn't enjoy taking orders from you."

Deborah, retrieving a slender cigarette from her handbag, let out a hearty laugh that echoed against the backdrop of the rolling waves. "He has no choice but to take orders from me," she declared confidently.

"How so?" Doyle asked, genuinely curious.

In response, Deborah exhaled a thick plume of white smoke that curled and danced in the air, transforming into an intricate image of a kraken, its tentacles undulating gracefully as if alive. With a twinkle in her eye and a tone that blended pride with playful mischief, she declared, "I am his mother."

Doyle's eyes widened in disbelief as he dropped his cigar, the ember glowing briefly in the deck lighting. "You're his what?" he stammered, trying to wrap his mind around the revelation.

Deborah met his astonished gaze, her expression resolute. "He is my and Edward's son. Can you not see how he wields such authority in this realm? Everything he has orchestrated up to this point has been with one purpose: to capture his father and bring him to face judgment in Atlantis, where the ancient powers will weigh his sins."

Doyle picked his cigar off the deck, shaking his head in disbelief. "Wait a minute. Are you a prisoner or not?"

"I am indeed," she admitted, her tone growing serious as she gazed thoughtfully into the distance. "I find myself imprisoned for the crimes I committed in a past life. It was Jonah who played a crucial role in aiding the Patriots Group to track me down and ultimately bring me here, confined to the damp sewer district. A death warrant was on my head, yet Jonah, driven by a sense of loyalty or perhaps a flicker of compassion for his mother, chose to spare my life."

Doyle sat in silence, absorbing every word coming from Deborah. "After spending several decades ensnared in this elaborate facade of confinement, I arrived at a difficult but necessary decision: to lend my support to my son and his group, the Patriots Group. Their mission is one I believe in with unwavering conviction: to seek out and capture the hybrids that disrupt our world, leaving a trail of chaos and destruction in their wake. This undertaking is fraught with danger, given the formidable nature of these hybrids and the hostility they often exhibit, but I am ready to embrace it. I do so in the hope of correcting the mistakes of my past and contributing to a cause that promises to restore order and safety to our lives."

"So, does Edward know that Jonah is his son?" Doyle inquired, his brow furrowing with concern.

Deborah shook her head slowly, a hint of sadness in her eyes. "No, he doesn't. I made the difficult decision to hide Jonah in the known world, far away from this place, when he was just a small child. One of my dearest friends took him in and raised him in California. They not only taught him the unique abilities that come with being a hybrid but also guided him in learning how to navigate life among humans, helping him blend in seamlessly with their ways."

Doyle took a slow drag from his cigar, the smoke curling up into the cool night air as he gazed out at the luminous moon rising over the vast, undulating ocean. "When did Jonah finally understand who you truly were?" he inquired, his voice carrying a blend of curiosity and concern.

Deborah sighed softly, her eyes shimmering in the silvery light of the moon. "He was around eight years old when we had to sit him down and explain the truth about his origins," she recalled, her tone growing somber and filled with nostalgia. "That moment was a turning point for us. I realized that would be the last time I could visit him; the risks were too great. Edward would stop at nothing in his relentless pursuit to track me down, desperate to find his lost son."

"How long were you and Jonah apart?" Doyle inquired, his curiosity evident in his voice.

With a cigarette delicately balanced between her lips, Deborah replied, "Fifty long years."

"Damn!" Doyle exclaimed, his eyes widening in disbelief. "That's an incredibly long time."

Deborah offered a wistful smile, her gaze drifting toward the horizon where the ocean kissed the stars. “Not for a hybrid,” she replied, her voice tinged with the wisdom of her experiences, the weight of untold stories hanging delicately in the air between them.

They settled back, the quiet crackle of the cigarette between them blending with the soothing sound of waves lapping against the ship. The moon hung low in the sky, casting a silver glow over the water that shimmered like a blanket of stars. They remained there for a serene hour, completely absorbed in the beauty of the moment until the gentle rhythm of the night lulled Doyle to sleep.

Deborah, glancing down at him, felt a rush of affection. She leaned in and pressed a soft kiss on his forehead, the warmth of her touch lingering. “You are a darling,” she whispered, her words barely a breeze in the stillness of the night, before she turned and gracefully walked back to her suite, leaving the peaceful landscape to wrap around him like a comforting embrace.

A gentle jolt startled Doyle awake, pulling him from a deep sleep. “Sir, it’s time to rise and prepare your belongings. The shimmering lights of Atlantis are just ahead,” Eddie the drone announced, hovering near Doyle’s shoulder and nudging him gently to gain his attention.

Doyle slowly blinked his eyes open, trying to shake off the remnants of his slumber. “Wow, I really zonked out. How long was I asleep?” he asked, still feeling the weight of fatigue in his voice.

"Around five hours, sir," Eddie replied with his usual calm tone, his mechanical eyes scanning the horizon for a clearer view of their approaching destination.

Doyle stood up from his seat with a determined look. "I'm on it, Eddie. Give me a few minutes to gather my things," he said, striding purposefully toward his cabin, the sound of his footsteps echoing softly on the deck.

Meanwhile, the deckhands sprang into action, moving swiftly around the ship like a well-oiled machine, preparing for the tugboat that would assist in guiding the vessel safely to the dock. The Driver emerged onto the bridge deck, his keen eyes scanning the bustling activity below as he took charge of the operation.

"You did a fantastic job, Captain," Deborah remarked, approaching him with a warm smile. Two AI deckhands trailed behind her, effortlessly maneuvering her bags with precision and care.

"Thanks, Deborah. Just another successful mission under our belt," The Driver responded, his voice filled with a sense of accomplishment.

"I will ensure that a replacement captain is assigned to this ship as soon as I return to the Warden's office," Deborah explained, her expression turning serious. "Please instruct the crew that you will be disembarking from the vessel once they have it securely moored at the dock."

Doyle felt the ship gently rock as the powerful tugboat pushed it toward the bustling dock. Exiting the cabin, he closed the door behind him and spotted Sonny making his way through the throng of crew members and equipment, a warm smile on his face.

"Doyle, I just wanted to express how much I appreciated serving alongside you," Sonny said, extending his hand for a firm shake.

"Thank you, Sonny. I felt the same way," Doyle replied, meeting Sonny's gaze with genuine warmth.

They ascended the stairs to the deck, where the busy deckhands were in the midst of lowering the heavy ramp, allowing for the disembarkation of the crew. As they reached the top, Deborah approached Doyle with a radiant smile. "Walk with me, darling," she said, intertwining her arm with his as they made their way down the ramp together.

At the bottom, Jonah and Mike stood waiting, their expressions a mix of excitement and bittersweet farewell.

"It's great to see you both," Jonah said, extending his hand for a hearty handshake.

"Jonah, Doyle has decided to take an extended vacation and has requested that his dog, Gunner, be brought to Atlantis to live with him and Susan," Deborah explained, clearly proud of the decision Doyle had made.

Jonah turned to Doyle, his expression serious yet understanding. "I hate to lose your skills and expertise, but I completely understand. Just let me know what you need, and I'll make it happen."

With a smile, Deborah turned to Doyle and wrapped her arms around him in a warm hug. "It's truly been an honor getting to know you. Please make sure to come visit me sometime."

"Thank you, Deborah. If you could send me a few tickets, we would love to see one of your shows as Miss Candy," Doyle replied with a playful grin.

Deborah laughed, a musical sound that brightened the atmosphere. "I don't think Susan would appreciate me as Miss Candy," she said with a wink.

"You're probably right," Doyle responded, chuckling along with her.

He then made his way over to a waiting flying taxi, calling out to his trusty drone, Eddie. "This way, buddy! You're going to be living with us now!"

Eddie, the agile drone, swiftly soared through the air and settled neatly in the open door that Doyle held. Just before stepping into the taxi, Doyle turned back for one last glance at the ship. "If I hadn't witnessed all of this firsthand, I would have a hard time believing it was real," he murmured to himself, a sense of wonder washing over him. "At least we figured out where the missing people were going, and we cut it off," he said to Jonah as he closed the door.

Deborah and Jonah stood at the edge of the dock, their eyes fixed on the fading tail lights of Doyle's flying taxi as it disappeared into the night. The air was heavy with the scent of salty sea breeze, mingling with the distant sounds of the bustling port. "Should we erase his memory and send him back to the States?" Jonah asked, casting a worried glance at Deborah.

Deborah remained silent for a moment, a tear glistening on her cheek as she weighed the gravity of their situation. "No," she finally replied, her voice steady but laced with emotion. "We should relocate them to the serene countryside of Atlantis and ensure they have round-the-clock security to keep them safe."

Mike, standing nearby, nodded in understanding. "I'll handle the arrangements for you, Jonah," he said, his tone reassuring.

Deborah turned her gaze back to the ramp, where deckhands were beginning to escort Edward off the ship, his expression a mixture of confusion and apprehension. "We're going to have our hands full with Edward," she remarked, anticipating the challenges that lay ahead in managing the delicate circumstances surrounding him.

CHAPTER TWELVE

EDWARD TO PRISON

0410 HOURS
PRESENT-DAY
THE SHIPYARD DISTRICT, ATLANTIS

Edward stood defiantly near the top of the ramp, his voice echoing with indignation. "This is an unlawful arrest!" he shouted, the tension in the air thick. Jonah, glancing over with a smirk, couldn't help but comment, "Oh my, I didn't realize he was so short," a statement he relayed to Deborah as the imposing AI security guards marched up the ramp, their precise, unwavering movements automated. They approached Edward, swiftly taking control and guiding him toward the waiting flying police van, the distant hum of its engine filling the air.

As they led him off the ship and past Deborah, Edward turned his head with a desperate look in his eyes. "Come see me, babe," he implored, a hint of vulnerability beneath his bravado.

Deborah, however, only smiled, her expression both teasing and dismissive. "I don't like short men," she replied coolly, her tone leaving no room for misinterpretation.

In a surge of anger, Edward lunged forward, his frustration boiling over. "You did this to me! I'll show you!" he shouted, the determination in his voice overshadowed by the inevitability of his capture.

In an instant, the AI security team sprang into action, expertly pushing Edward to the ground. One guard delivered a sharp punch to his ribs, eliciting a sharp scream from him as pain coursed through his body. They flipped him onto his back, their movements unfaltering and methodical, before helping him to his feet once again.

With a determined stride, Deborah approached him, her expression fierce as she stood unflinchingly close. "Call me babe again," she challenged him, her voice low and threatening, "And I'll end you right here." The intensity of her gaze locked onto his, conveying a message that left no doubt about her resolve.

The security team carefully placed Edward inside the sturdy van, ensuring they had him securely restrained, then climbed in themselves. The vehicle's engine roared to life, and it pulled away from the bustling city shipyard, heading toward the elevator to the Sewer District and then the grim confines of the prison.

Meanwhile, Deborah approached Jonah, handing him a long, weathered box with a determined expression. "Here is my staff for you to lock up," she said, her voice steady despite the situation.

Jonah accepted the box with a nod, understanding the weight of her request. "Absolutely. I can't allow you to keep that in the Sewer

District," he replied, glancing around to ensure their privacy as they walked toward a nearby taxi. The air was thick with tension, but he tried to maintain a sense of calm. "Deborah, I promise I will see you soon. I will make an effort to attend Edward's trial, but first, I need to help Doyle get settled into his new home out in the hills." The determination in his voice conveyed his commitment to support both of them in this challenging time.

"I know you will, Jonah," replied Deborah, her voice steady as she climbed into a sleek flying taxi, settling into the plush seat beside The Driver. Outside, the bustling cityscape blurred in a kaleidoscope of lights and colors. "It feels like we're back to being prisoners again," The Driver remarked softly, glancing at Deborah with a mixture of concern and determination.

Back in the dimly lit corridors of the Sewer District, Deborah stood on the balcony of the Warden's office, gazing intently as the security team meticulously unloaded Edward from a Sewer District police car. "Keep your filthy hands off me!" he shouted defiantly, his voice echoing off the damp walls as the guards began the laborious process of removing his chains.

Close by, a massive dragon, its scales shimmering in shades of emerald and gold, observed Edward with an intense gaze. "I never thought I would see you again, Edward," the dragon rumbled, its voice deep and resonant, filled with a mixture of nostalgia and malice.

Edward turned to face the imposing creature, his eyes narrowing in suspicion. "What wisdom can a dragon who cannot fly offer me?" he challenged.

The dragon stepped forward, its massive form casting a shadow over Edward. "My wings are shackled by unbreakable chains, binding me to this wretched place and preventing me from soaring through the skies," it explained, a hint of sorrow lacing its voice. "My dragon fire, once a force of destruction, lies dormant and cannot burn. But make no mistake, small human—I still possess the power to devour you like the mere snack you are," the dragon warned, baring its sharp teeth as it moved ever closer, the air crackling with tension between them.

Edward recoiled, his heart pounding in his chest, as the dragon's deep, rumbling voice echoed ominously through the dimly lit prison courtyard, casting eerie shadows on the cold stone walls. "What kind of snack would a man be with only half his legs?" it inquired, its enormous, scaled mouth twisting into a mischievous grin that glinted in the sparse light. The creature's laughter reverberated like distant thunder, sending a chill down Edward's spine and amplifying the oppressive atmosphere of dread.

"Your kind has always been vile creatures we should have eradicated from this world!" Edward retorted sharply, his voice laced with defiance and righteous anger as he stood firm against the monstrous being.

The dragon, its massive body straining against heavy iron chains, leaned closer, trying to bridge the gap between them. "We have relished feasting on the flesh of your kind," it sneered, its hunger palpable and unsettling. "Even humans put up a better fight than the likes of you hybrids."

"Funny, coming from a dragon trapped in metal shackles," Edward countered, a smirk creeping onto his face despite his fear.

The dragon's laughter boomed once more, echoing through the chamber. "But I am still free to roam outside in the relentless rain, while you, poor wretch, are confined to a dark, windowless cell. Even your father, Folly, cannot save you now."

"Keep my father's name out of your mouth, you foul beast!" Edward shouted, his voice rising to a furious pitch, fueled by a mixture of anger and desperation. The air crackled with tension as he braced himself for whatever retaliation the dragon might unleash.

Deborah grinned from her elevated vantage point as she observed the dragon playfully tormenting Edward below, its shimmering scales catching the light. With a graceful stride, she entered the sleek, modern office adorned with holographic displays. "Please arrange my flying bike," she instructed her AI assistant, her voice both authoritative and confident. "I'm eager to unwind at my bar and enjoy a well-deserved break." The AI assistant, with its soft, melodic tone, replied, "Certainly, ma'am," as it began processing her request.

As Deborah stepped back onto the balcony, awaiting her flying bike, the massive prison loomed below her, bathed in rain and fading light. Above the clamor of the bustling courtyard, she could hear the unmistakable sounds of chaos—the sharp roars of the dragon intertwined with Edward's frantic shouts. Leaning over the rough stone ledge of the towering warden's office, which loomed like a dark sentinel, she called down with a playful, mocking tone, "I hope you're settling in nicely in your new palace, Edward!"

Edward, momentarily distracted from his struggle, glanced up, surprise etched onto his face as he spotted her framed against the vibrant lights. "Why don't you come join me?" he retorted with a confident smirk, his voice echoing with a hint of bravado. "I hear you prefer having plenty of men around!"

With a resolute motion, Deborah signaled to the AI prison guards, whose mechanical forms stood rigid and imposing in their dark uniforms. The guards promptly moved to unshackle the dragon, their movements precise and efficient. Edward's expression shifted from bravado to dread as he realized the gravity of the situation. He began hopping awkwardly toward the formidable iron prison door, his heart racing.

In an instant, once the heavy chains fell away with a loud clank, the dragon sprang into action. Its massive wings unfurled, creating a gust that whipped through the courtyard, sending paper swirling into the air. With a powerful leap, it snatched Edward up in its formidable jaws, lifting him effortlessly as if he were a mere toy, before hurling him across the rain-soaked expanse of the prison courtyard.

"Help me!" Edward shouted, his voice trembling with desperation as he landed awkwardly on the muddy ground, dazed and disoriented. The dragon, a magnificent creature with iridescent scales that shimmered in the light of the flickering courtyard torches, advanced toward him with a predatory grace. A slow, menacing smile stretched across its fearsome face, revealing rows of sharp, glistening teeth. "Now, what do you have to say, little man?" it taunted, looming over him with an aura of unrestrained dominance, its piercing eyes sparkling with wicked amusement.

With trembling hands raised in a gesture of surrender, Edward pleaded, "Please, do not eat me!"

The dragon studied him for a moment, its nostrils flaring as it inhaled deeply. "What do I smell? Did you wet your pants?" it teased, a cruel twist in its voice.

"Enough!" Deborah exclaimed, her authoritative tone cutting through the tension in the air. "Now is not the time for death. Once the court convicts him to life in this prison, I give you my word, you may feast on his flesh."

"What?" Edward shouted in disbelief, desperation flooding his voice as he turned to her, his eyes wide and panicked.

"As you wish, my lady," the dragon responded, its tone dripping with mockery as it bowed its massive head in acknowledgment. The guards, moving swiftly, led the dragon back to its chains, securing it with heavy iron links that clanked ominously in the stillness of the courtyard.

Still covered in mud and the remnants of his earlier terror, Edward was hoisted to his feet by the guards, who walked him toward the looming entrance of the prison. The heavy iron door creaked open, revealing the dark and foreboding interior.

"See you in a year or so when your trial starts!" Deborah shouted after him, her voice echoing through the cold, stone corridor as the prison door slammed shut behind Edward, sealing his fate in the oppressive darkness.

Deborah turned to her assistant, a confident smile curling at the corners of her lips, and said, "I'm ready for a drink. With Doyle gone,

I'm going to resume my role as the Bartender. It's time to reestablish my rules here in the Sewer District." She paused momentarily, taking in the scene around her. The dim lighting cast a flickering glow, struggling to penetrate the dense, rainy haze that enveloped the area. At the same time, her expressive eyes sparkled with a blend of authority and playful mischief. Outside on the balcony, her sleek flying bike gleamed under the few scattered lights, poised for a swift escape into the stormy sky.

Slipping into her well-worn raincoat and securing her helmet, Deborah climbed onto the flying bike with practiced ease. As she elevated from the platform, she expertly maneuvered the bike down the steep incline, landing gracefully in the rain-slicked courtyard of the decrepit prison. The cool, refreshing droplets fell against her skin like tiny kisses, invigorating her as she approached the imposing dragon that loomed nearby, its massive form towering over her. With scales that shimmered like wet obsidian in the dim light, the dragon exuded an aura of both danger and loyalty. Featuring a sharp-toothed grin, it eagerly accepted a generous piece of meat that Deborah offered, the savory aroma mixing with the scent of rain in the air.

"Thank you, Deborah. I was delighted to follow the instructions you sent me earlier to keep Edward on his toes," it rumbled in a low, gravelly voice that resonated through the courtyard.

"You have always treated me well," Deborah said, stroking the dragon's snout affectionately, feeling the warmth radiate from its hearty form, a stark contrast to the chill of the rain. The bond between them was profound, formed through trust and shared adventures.

With a satisfied smile stretching across her face, she climbed back onto the flying bike, her heart racing with anticipation. As the bike lifted off from the slick cobblestone courtyard and soared high into the rain-filled sky, it swiftly vanished over the towering prison walls. The heavy rain continued to drum against the bike's surface, a rhythmic reminder of the exhilaration that marked yet another daring chapter in her unpredictable life.

THE END

www.ingramcontent.com/pod-product-compliance
Lightning Source LLC
LaVergne TN
LVHW090604110826
845146LV00001B/258

* 9 7 9 8 9 9 4 1 4 5 2 2 7 *